THE TELLING

Anne Wolf

Cover Art Design by: Kelly Moran/Rowan Prose Publishing

Photo Credit: Adobe Images/Deposit Photos

First Edition

ISBN: 978-1-961967-70-0

Rowan Prose Publishing, LLC

www.RowanProsePublishing.com

Published in the United States of America

Acknowledgments:

In a project such as this, there are always people who deserve thanks and gratitude, and there are many ways to offer help. First, I send love and give thanks to my husband, Irv Wolf, who gave his full-throated support to all of my endeavors and projects throughout the years. He has been a dedicated reader and cheerleader who read all my revisions patiently, asked for explanations and clarifications where needed, and always encouraged my dreams.

My daughter, Jennifer Wolf Kam, an inspiring author in her own right, was also a significant help in teaching me how to navigate the publishing process and the Book World in general. Jen was there to answer my many questions about the industry when I didn't know where to begin, to read much of my work, and to answer my questions about technology. She is my Halloween spirit-sister, and we both enjoy all aspects of that holiday!

My son, Michael, who taught me to see the world through different eyes. My grandsons, Zachary, a whirlwind force of nature, and Ben, who loves scary movies and says I ask too many questions, are both inspirations. Jason Kam, the best son-in-law anyone could ask for, was cooperative, helpful, and selfless, despite his own busy schedule.

My sister, Susan Helene Nack, author of two short story collections, helped me with more than one technology problem. She knew how to apply different strategies to various situations on the computer and was generous in sharing them. She was constantly encouraging and is head of the West Coast boosters (Jaime and Adina included) who were always there to cheer me on! My brother, Dr. Bruce Schneider, also provided helpful assistance with technology. He is now beginning his own writing journey.

I couldn't have written "The Telling" in its present form without the assistance of special beta readers and techies. This group includes Jennifer Wolf Kam, Barbara Mogelof, (who was a big help with marketing and promotional tasks as well) Beryl Fischer, Margo Messina, Elaine Healy, Donna Kornblatt, Gail Brown, and Dotty Sabatino. These amazing people were beta readers for "The Telling." Dotty also helped me with a very sticky technology problem that made it difficult for me to send out my work.

She used her magic and expertise to solve the problem—incredible! Special thanks, too, to Gary Whittier for his help with technology.

Another helpful and talented group is the SCBWI critique group of writers on Long Island, led by Maria Wen Adcock. All the members are supportive of each other, but I must single out a few who offered valuable insights and suggestions from the early days of "The Telling." They are: Maria Wen Adcock, Elyse Trevers, Anthony Baldasare, Stephen Martin, and later, Patricia Brown. Thank you all for helping me make my paranormal YA mystery/thriller ready for publication. To David Fry, big thanks for your encouragement and support as well. To all of you, your ability to think outside the box was helpful beyond measure.

A big thank you to everyone at Rowan Prose Publishing. You have all been wonderful, believing in the potential of this story, and turning the manuscript into a real book! Kelly Moran, co-founder and my editor at Rowan Prose, has been so professional, organized, and focused. She kept me on task and was always totally supportive.

And last, but not least, the rest of my family, whose encouragement in all of my endeavors lifts me up and inspires me to seek new challenges. I love you all!

A note of appreciation goes to all the librarians, booksellers, and teachers, who do so much to encourage reading and a love of literature. I value all of you!

DEDICATION:

This book is dedicated to the memory of my parents, Sally and George Schneider, who always had confidence in me and spurred me on to seek new challenges. I feel their presence with me—always—guiding me with their love.

A message to all aspiring writers: Don't give up. You need perseverance, self-confidence, and courage to climb the mountain. You'll get to the top one way or another if you are determined and believe in yourself. Surround yourself with positive influencers and join at least one critique group. The sharing of ideas and suggestions is invaluable and will help you grow as a writer.

Prologue

Five years earlier...

Most ten-year-old girls *do not* have to bury their mothers.

Maeve Newell peeked through the heavy velvet curtains that separated the chapel from a second, private room. She saw her father push his way into the room where her mother's casket rested. He was hysterical, out of his mind with grief. He tried to pry open the casket, but the undertaker stopped him.

"Let me see her!" James Newell yelled, the tears merging with the thick mucus dripping from his nose as the funeral director and his assistant tried to pull him away from the sealed coffin. The intensity of his behavior frightened Maeve.

The funeral director turned to James Newell. "Your father has already confirmed the identity of the deceased. There's not much left of her. Better to remember her as she was in life," he continued.

Maeve was just a few feet away and heard the complete conversation, not meant for her young ears. James let out an agonizing scream and crumpled to the floor.

Ten-year-old girls who *do* have to bury their mothers, don't think of the corpse as mutilated. They imagine their mother as whole, just as they last saw her. *What parts were missing? Did she still have two eyes?* She hadn't even considered that her mother would no longer look like the woman who cradled her in her gentle arms when Maeve was troubled or scared. Maeve wanted to look upon her one last time, but the undertaker's words frightened her, compounding the trauma of her loss. Her father's lack of control increased her fear and sadness. Maeve backed away from "*the room,*" shrinking into a corner pew in the chapel, fighting the urge to flee. Her grandfather, Papa Will, slid into the space next to her and put his arm around her shoulder. Although Maeve welcomed the gesture of support, it did nothing to remove the chill from the chapel or the ache in her heart.

Maeve was never more alone. Her father was inconsolable and unable to focus on his daughter's needs. Her mother, who was her chief supporter, was gone. Maeve had few friends, so the only children at the funeral were those who belonged to her mother's friends. Everything in Maeve's life revolved around her mom. *Gone. Murdered. Who did this to her?* Maeve couldn't get the disturbing details of her mother's death out of her head. It was not a natural death. She could not wrap her mind around what was taking place here. It was as though Maeve floated above the crowd, out of her body, watching.

Only her grandfather was there for her. She was grateful for his presence. He whispered to her as he patted her shoulder, "There, there, Maeve. You'll get through this. You've got Newell blood flowing through your veins."

I doubt it will help. Still, it was reassuring.

Across the room, Maeve recognized her mother's dearest friend, Nelda. Instead of approaching Maeve and offering her condolences, she appeared to be staring intently at Papa Will, looking like she could bore two deep holes in his skull with her eyes. The stormy expression on her face unsettled Maeve.

"Why is Nelda staring at you with that angry look on her face?" Maeve asked her grandfather.

"Pay her no mind, Maeve," he answered. "She's upset about your mother's passing. Times like these bring up all kinds of feelings—turn you inside out."

Maeve reluctantly took her eyes off Nelda and turned to the front of the room, where her father was sobbing in the first row. She tried to concentrate on the eulogy for Alice Newell, her loving mother.

After the service, a stream of townspeople stopped by the family farm. Visitors delivered casseroles, pies, sympathy, and recollections of her mom. Whiskey, snuff, and Irish music permeated the atmosphere.

Maeve was amazed at the change in her grandfather. As soon as he left the funeral home, it was as if he had put the morning's events and the gruesome details of Alice's murder behind him, returning to his gregarious self. Papa Will held court amongst a group of his peers, regaling them with exaggerated tales of what Wren Falls was like when he first settled there years earlier. He spoke of legendary creatures and misdeeds, but 10-year-old Maeve was too young to pay much attention to his ramblings. She clung to her dog, Pooch, for comfort. He was a stray she found in the backyard, and when she wasn't with him, she spent her time daydreaming and reading fantasy and folklore stories.

Maeve's father carried on about what a saint Alice was. "She was too good for me," he cried. "I never deserved her."

It was on this day that James Newell's addiction to Irish whiskey went full bore into overdrive. After that, it was as if his daughter became invisible to him. *I might as well have gone to live with the fairies,* she sighed.

The people of Wren Falls are a superstitious and secretive lot. Generations passed down their folklore and beliefs. This core of beliefs binds the townspeople together and informs their behavior.

Too bad.

The gravediggers buried Alice Newell beneath the arms of her favorite old oak tree. She was fond of telling her daughter, "This old oak will likely outlive us all," and in her case, it did. Alice was only 47 years worn when an unknown predator viciously mauled her to death, shocking the townspeople and creating a cloud of fear that hung over the area. A neighbor discovered Alice's body floating face up in the nearby creek, a look of total horror stamped on her visage. He ran to the closest home, screaming for help, and called the police. The rest is history, or is it?

Maeve was unprepared for this new reality. In the beginning, she asked her father repeatedly, "Daddy, what really happened to Mommy?" but James Newell brushed aside the questions, and finally, Maeve stopped asking him.

One night, Maeve had a dream about her mother. They were having a picnic under Alice's favorite oak tree. Maeve looked out at the acres of farmland that seemed to stretch beyond the capacity of the human eye.

"It's so peaceful here, Mom. Nothing bad could ever happen here."

"Yes, it is," Alice agreed. "This land has been in the family for years. It's always been my favorite place to think, relax, and dream." She smiled lovingly at Maeve, who took her hand and gave it a gentle squeeze. At that moment, Maeve watched her mother begin to fade from view.

"Mom! Mom!" she shrieked. "Stop! Where are you going?"

"A-w-a-y-y-y-y, my darling girl!" Alice struggled to speak. Her voice took on an unreal, deep timbre as the words tumbled out in slow motion. It seemed to come from far away. Alice barely got out her words before dissolving right in front of Maeve's contorted face.

"Don't go, Mom!" cried Maeve, trying to grasp her mother's hand, but it was too late. Alice was gone, and Maeve was bereft. She awoke with a start. As she tried to focus her eyes on her surroundings, she noticed her tears had stained her blanket.

The dream had turned into a nightmare. It took several weeks for it to fade from Maeve's conscious mind, but it was never completely gone from her waking thoughts. She longed to understand its meaning. She couldn't explain why it kept coming to her, but it was definitely taking a toll on her health.

Maeve's father, James Makepeace Newell, was a man possessed of a very important-sounding name and little else. He tried resuming farming, but after Alice's demise, he lacked the inclination and stamina to rise at dawn to care for his crops or his animals. Failing that, he attempted to sell sets of the Britannica Encyclopedia door to door. The residents of Wren Falls, most beyond school age and barely eking out a living, were not predisposed to spend what seemed like a small fortune on the lives of Louis XIV or Julius Caesar. They politely declined James's pitch—another unsuccessful venture.

The brutal death of Alice Newell was the last straw for James, who became a ghost of his former self. A neighbor bought the farm from James, who moved with Maeve into a rickety old cottage that he purchased for a small sum. He spent his time working a still he constructed in the back-woods behind his cottage. James consumed much of its product himself. He was often seen stumbling around his home in an alcoholic stupor, muttering to himself. Sometimes, Maeve could even hear him talking to his dead wife.

"Alice," he would say to empty space, "I'm going out back now to work on the still. Please have dinner ready when I return. Hard work gives me quite an appetite." This frightened Maeve and she worried that he was losing his mind. Thirsty neighbors purchased the remaining whiskey. They were not particularly discerning.

Maeve's relationship with her father suffered mightily after her mother's death. It seemed he could only focus on his whiskey-making still. Nothing else seemed to occupy his thoughts, and he showed Maeve little or no affection. He assigned her all the housekeeping chores and barely talked to her. She was to clean the whole house, prepare meals, take care of Pooch and his needs, and complete all laundry chores as well. She was neglected and invisible to her father. She had no close friends, so she lived an isolated, lonely existence, except for the companionship of her loyal Pooch.

"You love me, boy, don't you?"

At that moment, Pooch would wave his tail joyfully and lick her eager face.

"That's my boy," Maeve said to the dog. "At least someone cares for me." And she would playfully scratch his back and give him a belly rub.

The one good thing Maeve got from her father was William Makepeace Newell or, as Maeve referred to him, "Papa Will." Her granddad lived down the road in a dirty, clapboard, one-bedroom home, until his death during Maeve's eleventh year. Papa Will's house sported a broken-down wraparound porch with Adirondack chairs in faded colors—some rockers, some not. Next to the porch was an open area that supported a decrepit wooden glider. This swing was a favorite spot where young Maeve listened to Papa Will's sanitized stories of Irish myths and legends.

"Tell me a story, Papa—one of the ancient myths, please," Maeve pleaded.

"I don't know, Maeve. It may be too scary for you," Papa teased.

"I can take it, Papa." Maeve would then add, "I've got Newell blood in my veins."

"That you have, girl. That you have," he chuckled. Then, he would choose one of his favorite tales to share. Wanting to ensure a love of Irish culture in his granddaughter, he left out the blood-curdling details of these dark tales and softened them for his beloved Maeve.

He did her no favor.

Papa Will was a man of small stature. His outsized personality made up for his slender, wiry frame, and he had a knack for storytelling. On many evenings, he entertained the patrons in Flannery's Bar and Grill with his tales far into the night, with no regard for the lateness of the hour. His ability to draw people to him was the quality Maeve most admired in him. *I wish I could be more like Grandpa,* she thought to herself and spent many hours in front of her bathroom mirror, trying to imitate his voice and gestures. Sometimes, Papa Will would catch her doing these imitations out of the corner of his eye, and he would hide behind the door, watching and grinning. He was crazy about his granddaughter, and the feeling was mutual.

Papa Will's death from a sudden heart attack left a huge void in her life. Maeve often visited his empty home to sit on the glider, and pretended to tell him the stories he shared with her when she was younger.

"Papa, today I'm going to tell you the story of Morrigan, the shapeshifter who could predict a person's death." Her mother's death was still very much on her mind. With Alice gone, a lonely young girl had only her alcoholic father, her dog, Pooch, and her imagination to keep her company.

Chapter 1

*F*ive *years later...*

As the Earth turned, summer disrobed and reclined, waiting for her lover with the icy hands. The moon took its place in the cloudless sky, and the Arctic chill from the north slithered in, squeezing Wren Falls, leaving it breathless.

It was on those nights that the old house's bones rattled until the wee hours of the morning when 15-year-old Maeve fell into a restless sleep. Small as the house was, it seemed crowded with the ghosts of those who had passed, whispering to her throughout the night. Maeve was aware of them all. The familiar, "Whoosh!" and the creepy shadows that appeared in the corners of her room, caused Maeve to pull her covers tightly around her tired body as she squeezed her eyes shut until sleep overtook her.

One late afternoon in December, Maeve took Pooch for his daily walk through the woods. These walks usually involved a short run after Pooch spied some stray birds who chose not to fly south or an errant squirrel readying itself for the coming winter. Without trepidation, Maeve ran after him as twilight wrapped around her and the moon ascended.

Maeve's loyal dog, Pooch, was her primary companion and friend. He was her lookout and protector as well. When Pooch growled, there was danger afoot. Living so close to the woods, bears, wolves, and other predators lurked nearby. When winter closed in, it was time to be extra vigilant, and Pooch seemed to sense that, warning her immediately if danger was near.

Suddenly, Pooch stopped dead in his tracks. His ears flattened back on his head, and a low growl escaped from his jaws. His back was ramrod straight. His head lowered for battle. Not a muscle moved.

"Pooch, what is it?" Maeve whispered. What's there, boy?"

She tightened her grip on the leash. Maeve looked up. just in time to notice a strangely shaped shadow flitting through the wooded area behind the large oaks. She couldn't quite make out what it was, but then a blood-curdling cry seemed to come from the bowels of the earth and shook her to her core. The hairs stood up on the back of her neck, and Pooch began to whimper.

Maeve tugged on his leash forcefully. "Come, Pooch. Home!"

The dog responded and began to run in the direction of the cottage, with Maeve following close behind. When she reached her house, Maeve threw open the front door, hurried in with her dog, and slammed it shut, locking the two of them inside, just in case–

Looking around, shivering from a combination of fear and adrenaline, Maeve noticed her father snoring on the couch, oblivious to what she experienced less than a mile from their home. With her heart still pounding, Maeve collapsed on her bed. Her limbs were shaking, and her throat was dry. "What *was* that thing?" she asked Pooch, not really expecting an answer.

That December afternoon's fright hid inside the recesses of Maeve's subconscious mind. It surfaced at night on numerous occasions, usually when Maeve was in a deep sleep and her father was not home. Alone, her mind went to very dark places. The dream intensified. That evening, she was again in the woods, a misshapen shadow running after her in and out of the oaks, hooves pounding on the hard ground. Sometimes, the shadow came close enough for Maeve to smell the foul breath of the creature and experience   the beast's hot breath burning the back of her neck. The snarling sounds coming from the monster terrified Maeve and her heartbeats pounded in sync with them. Running full out, Maeve never looked back. Thus, she never came face to face with the monster. For that, she was grateful.

Maeve woke up just as she was reaching the front door of her home in her nightmare and the creature's hooves were about to knock her to the ground. Breathless, her face dripping with sweat and her body shaking, Maeve called out to Pooch and let him sleep on her bed, giving her a false sense of protection. It was on these nights that Maeve wondered if she had imagined the monster and sincerely wished her pa had been home with her. As the days continued to get shorter and darkness overwhelmed Wren Falls, Maeve's walks with Pooch occurred earlier each day. She was not willing to press her luck and chance another run-in with the beast—real or imaginary. She did not confide in her father nor her "Aunt Nelda," who was the closest thing to a sister that Alice Newell ever had, even though they were not actually related. Maeve worried that her father would laugh at her and she would scare her "Aunt," who was a superstitious person to begin with. So, Maeve carried her burden silently, but it weighed heavily on her shoulders.

Maeve tried changing her route with Pooch at the end of the day. It took longer, but they avoided the woods. She hoped it would chase away her nightmares and the frightening images that plagued her. But they came repeatedly despite her new routine. She was getting little sleep each night, and her appetite was shrinking. She was a shadow of the girl she had been.

The rural town of Wren Falls, nestled in New York's Catskill Mountains, sat at the foot of a steep incline called Little Red Kill Hill. It was at the top of this road that Maeve's ramshackle cottage was located. The one hundred year old domicile had a slight tilt to it as if it was permanently in repose. The small town was settled in the 1800s by Irish and German immigrants—most of the street signs reminded its few visitors of that fact—and had been popular with skiing enthusiasts for a short time in the

1980s when the weather and the economy had contributed to a bustling winter hideaway. Skiers had flocked to nearby Hunter Mountain to enjoy the breathtaking vistas of the chairlift as they climbed to the summit in preparation for the downhill run.

Years later, in a reversal of fortune, the town went to seed. The economy tanked, and the weather stopped cooperating. The result was a largely deserted town, except for the locals, and a chairlift that had fallen into disuse owing to the lack of precipitation. Even the summer trade evaporated with the drought-like conditions. Fly fishing, swimming, and tubing became pastimes in the truest sense of the word. No one was interested in coming to Wren Falls when trendier, more modern vacation spots were available. Five minutes was enough time to traverse Main Street. All storefronts had dilapidated wooden signs in need of fresh paint.

One day, Maeve visited Papa Will's deserted home. She decided to explore the old attic. Ever since her grandpa died, Maeve wanted to tackle that project. *I wonder what Newell family treasures are in this old attic.* After about two hours of rummaging through piles of old clothes, broken dolls, mannequins, and such, she discovered a large book, more like a tome, covered in dust, entitled *The Encyclopedia of Celtic Lore.*

With a fearsome collection of creatures on the cover, it immediately piqued Maeve's curiosity. Thumbing through the pages, Maeve poured over the frightening image of Carman, the Celtic witch and Goddess of Dark Magic, who roamed the earth with her three evil sons, destroying anyone in their path. The Dullahan, the Irish ancestor of the Headless Horseman, who used a spinal column to spur on his horses, and the Dearg Due, a female vampire who rose yearly on the anniversary of the day she died to drain the blood from her latest victims, were there as well. Also in the collection was Morrigan, the Phantom Queen of Irish mythology, the shapeshifter who could transform herself into a crow or raven when foretelling someone's doom. Maeve's grandfather's softened descriptions of these legendary beings and their stories were in sharp contrast to the brutal portrayals in the book.

The monster that most captured Maeve's attention was the Questing Beast, a Celtic hybrid creature with the head of a snake, the body of a leopard, the backside of a lion, and the hooves of a deer. This monster had a cry like the bark of thirty wild dogs and terrified the inhabitants of the Irish countryside throughout the centuries. It was an old myth embedded in Irish culture and not spoken of in polite company.

"I bet the younger families in Wren Falls don't even know about it," Maeve said aloud. She returned the book to its resting place under a pile of old photographs in the attic for safekeeping. Maeve returned home to prepare a light supper for herself since her father would not return before her bedtime, which was a common occurrence.

Chapter 2

Maeve's schoolhouse was a twenty-minute walk through the woods from her home. It had two rooms—one for the younger children taught by Miss Renfro and one for the children who were eleven years of age and older, taught by Miss Clouder. There were only seven children in Maeve's class. Most of the older students had left to go to work to help support their families. Maeve was lucky in that regard. Her father was so often drunk that he rarely noticed her. He often left her up to her own devices.

Maeve was astonished when, one day in November, a new girl arrived at the school.

No one ever moved *into* Wren Falls. Most people moved *out* of it as soon as they could afford to, if ever. The girl was tall and bony, with startling blue eyes that lit up her face. She shyly made eye contact with Maeve, who motioned to the desk next to hers. Her seat was the one closest to the door.

"You can sit here," Maeve whispered to the new girl as Miss Clouder introduced her.

"Class, this is Sylvie Hoffmann. She just moved to Wren Falls from Kentucky, and I trust you will all welcome her."

Sylvie offered a weak smile while the rest of the class just stared. No one new had ever moved into this class, and the students were transfixed. Maeve shared her textbook with Sylvie, who murmured, "Thanks." At lunchtime, they sat together under a gnarled birch tree, eating together and getting acquainted.

Maeve learned that Sylvie's father had been a horse trainer, but the owner of the stables died, the horses were sold, and Mr. Hoffmann went north to look for employment. It was just Mr. Hoffmann and Sylvie. His wife had passed from cancer, and his young son had fallen from a horse and died last year. Sylvie and her dad just had each other, besides her grandma, Amelia Hoffmann, who remained in Kentucky. Mr. Hoffmann found work at an old mill about two miles out of town and hoped to find a home and a fresh start in Wren Falls.

The unexpected arrival of a potential friend was exciting for Maeve. Time spent with Sylvie taught her soon enough that a real friendship was not immediately in the offing. Sylvie was not particularly communicative. She didn't make eye contact with any of the other students, nor did she share her feelings freely, as Maeve came to realize when they ate lunch together over the next few weeks. An invisible wall surrounded her that was difficult to penetrate.

Winter arrived with its frosty mien—hibernation was in place. The days were shorter and darker. The walk through the woods was chilling, and Maeve shuddered at the stillness that enveloped her as she made her way home from school.

Maeve's relationship with Sylvie progressed slowly. They ate lunch together every day and exchanged polite conversation about insignificant matters. Sylvie kept her emotions in check, and Maeve didn't want to pressure her. She hoped to turn Sylvie's acquaintance into a true friendship, but was aware that would take a very long time. Maeve wanted to find the courage to share the December event with Sylvie but was afraid Sylvie would consider her insane. Maeve didn't want to lose this new relationship.

One winter day, Miss Clouder assigned the girls a joint project—researching legends of the area. Sylvie and Maeve understood they would need to work together on the assignment after school. There was no traditional library in Wren Falls. There was, however, a library in the local branch of the Historical Society in Wren Falls, above the Wren Falls laundromat, that specialized in artifacts and articles related to the town's history.

"Why don't we go to the Historical Society library after school?" Sylvie suggested. "Maybe they have some information that we can use for our report."

"Good idea."

"But I want to leave by five p.m. I need to start dinner for my pa."

What she didn't say was that she was afraid to walk home after dark. Sylvie was okay with Maeve's explanation, so the two girls planned to head out to the little library on the following day.

There were not many books on the subject of local legends at the Historical Society. There were, however, news articles dating back over a century chronicling bizarre events, sightings, and macabre crimes in the town.

"Oh, my God!" Sylvie pointed to a news story about a reported creature sighting only eight years earlier. She turned to Maeve. "Do you think this really happened?"

Maeve skimmed the article, her face pale as she read the details. "I don't know," she said slowly, "but it probably wouldn't be in the newspaper if it didn't, right?"

"This is so creepy," Sylvie went on. "I don't think Miss Clouder had this in mind when she assigned our project."

Regaining her composure, Maeve said, "You know, my grandpa had a big book of ancient Celtic myths in his attic. I used to spend hours reading it. Maybe we should check out that book for information. I remember it was really interesting, but also, parts of it were very scary."

"I'm game," agreed Sylvie. "Why don't we go over there tomorrow after school?"

"Okay, deal," answered Maeve. *Maybe I'll finally be able to share my secret with someone instead of carrying it around all by myself.* The girls collected their things and headed out of the Historical Society for their respective homes.

That night, Maeve flopped down into her bed, exhausted but also exhilarated. The possibility of having a friend to do things with was something she had wanted for as long as she could remember. The opportunity to collaborate on a subject that held a particular fascination for her was even more appealing. She couldn't wait to share Papa Will's book with Sylvie. At last, someone her own age would be on the same page, no pun intended, with her. She closed her eyes, eager for a good night's sleep.

The dream slammed into her with a vengeance. This time, a loud hissing sound, followed by a deafening roar came closer to her as she approached her home.

She screamed, "Papa Will, save me!"

The creature didn't slow its pace. It seemed intent on attacking her and God knows what else. Maeve's own panting filled her ears. Her legs were jelly. She could barely breathe. The opportunity to reach safety was quickly slipping away.

"Papa Will, help me, please!" she cried, but there was no response from her granddad.

She didn't dare look behind her. Her shoulder burned from the monster's hot breath. The growling became louder and more persistent. The beast's jaws snapped wildly as it reached for her.

Just at that moment, a crushing weight pressed down on her body and Maeve was sure she was about to die. It was only Pooch's wail that woke her. He lay on her abdomen, trying to bring her back from the depths of the abyss.

Chapter 3

The next day, Sylvie accompanied Maeve to Papa Will's house, which, although deserted, was unlocked. Maeve retrieved the old book from the attic, and the two girls sat down to check out the Celtic monsters and creatures of the ancient myths and legends. Sylvie was fascinated.

"I had no idea there were so many Celtic creatures and myths," her eyes popping in amazement.

"Yes," agreed Maeve. "These were all the stories Papa Will told me when I was growing up, only he left out the really scary parts." She laughed.

Sylvie's eyes continued to bulge as she read several of the old Celtic stories with Maeve, who was thrilled to note Sylvie's interest. For Maeve, it was a review and an opportunity to share her culture with a friend. Time passed quickly, and soon, dusk had settled in.

"Uh oh." Maeve sat up with a start as she glanced outside. "We'd better get going."

She grabbed the old book, raced up to the attic, replaced it under the stack of old photos, and waved good-bye to Sylvie.

"Don't go near the woods, Sylvie, and stick to the main road so you don't get lost." Then, feeling a pang of guilt that she hadn't warned Sylvie about the beast, she added, "There are dangerous animals in those woods. You'd be better off taking the roads instead. It's a longer walk, but it's safer."

"Okay!" Sylvie yelled back to her as Maeve sprinted home, hoping Sylvie would get home safely.

The trip home was blessedly uneventful. Maeve was grateful until Pooch, greeted her with his leash hanging forlornly from his mouth. As the sun began to set, Maeve reluctantly took Pooch outside for a quick walk around the property, fearful of going too far afield and constantly scanning her surroundings.

From a distance, Maeve's ears were assaulted by the cries of what sounded like dozens of barking dogs. Pooch paced back and forth outside the front door, pulling the leash taught. He began to tremble. Maeve rushed him inside the house, and just as she pulled on the doorknob to close the entryway, she caught a glimpse of a distorted shape flitting in and out of the nearest cluster of trees. It moved clumsily, loping along with an erratic gait. It turned, stopping to stare in the direction of Maeve and Pooch for a long moment. Maeve shivered in spite of the fact that the weather was mild. She locked the door, closed the curtains, and crouched behind her torn sofa, praying that her father would be home soon and that the unidentified, frightening beast would disappear. Pooch stood guard, growling at her feet. Maeve hoped her father wouldn't meet up with the mysterious creature on his way home. The monster who had appeared in her grandfather's book was disturbingly *real*.

The month of January was brutally cold. The snowfall broke all modern records in Wren Falls, going back more than a century. No one left home unless they had to, and the eerie silence that descended upon the area was unsettling.

The schoolchildren were still on winter break. Maeve and Sylvie had not seen each other since before Christmas—when they handed in their project on myths and legends of the area. Maeve missed the relationship that was developing between them and was eager for the mounds of snow to disappear. She was bored and tired of being housebound. It was even impossible to visit Papa Will's dilapidated homestead. There were no passable roads or paths. The only good thing about conditions in the community was that Maeve's pa was experiencing a period of forced sobriety. The still was shut down, and he had nowhere to go and drink. He was sullen, sober, and not much of a conversationalist. Nevertheless, Maeve tried.

"Hey, Pa. D'ya wanna help me shovel a path outside our front door?"

"Nah. It'll all melt in time—waste of energy," Pa replied, supine on the sofa.

"How 'bout taking a walk with Pooch and me' round the outside of the house? He needs to go out."

"Ain't got good boots for any old snow walk," he answered.

"C'mon, Pa," Maeve pleaded.. "Let's do *something.*"

"Stop yer yammerin'," Pa answered. "Lemme be before I lose my temper."

And that would be the way most of their talks went. Finally, Maeve would don her worn winter clothes and take Pooch outside for a stroll.

One particularly bitter morning, the winds bending the boughs of the trees almost to the ground, Maeve took Pooch outside for his morning walk. Her feet plunged into the high snowbanks, challenging her to put one snow-laden foot in front of the other. Pooch sank into the snow, moving forward with great difficulty. It was not a day for a leisurely walk, and the two of them were soon anxious to retreat back into the warmth of the cottage.

As Maeve and Pooch headed back to the front door, they spied huge hoof prints pressed into the snow. *These don't look like they belong to any animal from around here,* Maeve reflected. *They're too big for our local deer.* She noticed, too, that the hooves were uneven. One side left deeper prints than the other. The crisp air carried the cries of a pack of wild dogs through the blanketed woods to their home. Maeve turned toward the sound, a chill running down her back. Pooch's ears flattened, and he emitted a low growl. Nearby, a louder growl responded. Maeve tugged on his leash and called out, "Pooch, inside. *Now!*"

The terrified girl high-stepped through the deep snow into the cottage entryway, shaken and angry that her father couldn't be bothered clearing a path for them. Maeve sensed that real danger had entered Wren Falls, but she pushed it out of her mind and tried to concentrate on more pleasant things.

Uncharacteristically, February arrived with a brief warming trend. Temperatures climbed into the forties, and the mountains of snow began to morph into puddles of water. School had reopened, and Maeve was thrilled at the possibility of reconnecting with Sylvie.

Even though the girls had finished their project for Miss Clouder, they were eager to revisit *The Encyclopedia of Celtic Lore* at Papa Will's house after school the next day. The ancient myths and folklore fascinated them.

"I can't wait to read some more of those spooky stories," Sylvie admitted.

"Right. They're not like any other stories I've ever read. Sylvie, have you had any bad dreams since we started reading the stories in this book?"

"Why, Maeve?"

"Just wonderin'. Sometimes my imagination gets carried away, and I dream about these creatures," Maeve confided.

"Nope. That hasn't happened yet, but who knows? It could one day."

The girls finished their peanut butter and jelly sandwiches, chocolate milk, and bananas, cleaned up, and hurried back into the classroom, where Miss Clouder was beginning her social studies lesson. Miss Clouder was always punctual and insisted that her students be the same. She was also very concerned about protecting the environment and required the students to clean up after themselves. No one wanted to cross her on either of these matters.

Chapter 4

In an earlier life, Maeve's grandpa, William Makepeace Newell, arrived in Salem, Massachusetts, in December 1689 after an Atlantic crossing from Donnelly, Ireland. Prior to his voyage, his wife, Megan O'Brien, had accidentally died from a fall down the steep stairs of their old stone house, breaking her neck. The last thing she saw before taking that fateful last step was a large black bird sitting on her windowsill, returning her glance with a most singular stare. Megan, distracted by the intensity of the bird's regard, lost her footing, ending the idyllic marriage permanently. Will and Megan had no children, and after a respectable period of mourning, William resolved that he needed to start a new life in a new country, far from whispering neighbors and prying eyes.

A rough voyage landed his wobbly sea legs on the coast of Massachusetts, where he began the journey northward to the religious community of Salem. Alone, with only a knapsack containing some ale and stale bread to sustain him, he found odd jobs in the town and a place to board at Goody Webster's modest abode. She, who baked bread and sweets for the townspeople, was also a crafter of charms and potions on the side for those who believed in her powers. She had a thriving trade and was happy to train William in the finer points of her Light Magic. William and Goody

Webster formed a close bond and shared secrets that were unknown to others.

Among her possessions was a book called *The Codex Demonicus*, handed down to Goody by her ancient Irish grandmother. On the evening of February 16, 1692, Goody Webster was arrested, accused of practicing witchcraft, and put through a two-week trial, wherein she was accused of all kinds of heinous deeds and eventually pronounced *Guilty*. Her punishment was death by hanging on a hill east of the town, two days after the verdict. William visited her while she awaited her fate, and from under her bedclothes, Goody pulled out her book. Looking furtively around for eavesdroppers, Goody whispered, "Guard this book with your life, William. My grandmother, Moira, the Grand Witch of the East, gave it to me two millennia ago. It holds the secrets of all the evils in the world. I've watched over this book since my youth and have kept the monsters and creatures at bay for hundreds of years. It is my time now to rejoin the earth, and I must pass this book on to one that I trust."

William's eyes bulged with recognition. "You mean me?" he asked in shock.

"Yes," she answered. "There is no one else to whom I can entrust this compendium of Evil. The world's very existence will depend upon you."

William gingerly took the heavy tome from her gnarled fingers and hid it under his long coat.

"In return," Goody added, "You will receive the blessing of longevity as I have. You will live hundreds of years longer than any other human. You will learn much and live many lifetimes. You will have longevity but not immortality. The time will come eventually when your life will end, like any other mortal." William could not believe what he was hearing.

"There is one other matter," continued Goody Webster. "The personal cost of guarding these evil spirits and creatures is that you will not be able to produce any of your own children. It would be too dangerous for them to live with you under these conditions. They would be vulnerable and prey for these monsters."

"No children?" William had always wanted a son to carry on his family name.

"No. I'm sorry," Goody went on. "There is no other way. Now, leave me be. I must prepare for my death on the morrow."

"I will do as you ask. God bless you, Goody Webster, and may you find peace in the next world."

"God bless you, as well, William." With that, she turned away, chanting in the darkest corner of her cell.

As Goody Webster had promised, William Makepeace Newell did live many lifetimes in his new country of America. Unfortunately, his wives did not. He began his new life in Salem as a simple carpenter and married Miss Abigail Williams in 1701. On October 31st, a stray ember from the fireplace in the living room ignited the rug, and fire engulfed their simple home. Abigail just caught a last glimpse of a large raven staring at her from a tree limb outside her window before thick black smoke rendered her unconscious. The approaching flames consumed her.

The fire occurred during Samhain, a three-day, three-night Celtic festival that marked the end of the summer and the start of the Celtic New Year. It was the end of October and the beginning of the cold, dark winter, a time associated with human death. People believed the barrier between the living and the dead was permeable during this time, and the ghosts of the dead returned to Earth. Citizens lit bonfires at the festival and wore costumes to scare off the ghosts. Abigail was a superstitious woman, and the rituals of the festival made her very uneasy. She stayed home to finish some sewing instead of accompanying William to the bonfire. As everyone was at the festival, there was no one to help poor Abigail. All that remained of her was a smoldering pile of her ashes. Because her death occurred during Samhain, eyebrows were raised in the suspicious town of Salem.

After a lengthy period of grieving, Will married Miss Eleanor Briggs in 1715, a wealthy widow with a love of all things horse-related. Will purchased three beautiful steeds for her to ride. One was a roan, another a dapple gray, and the third was a spirited two-year-old ebony stallion. On October 31, 1722, Eleanor rode the stallion into an unfamiliar meadow. A huge black bird spied her from a thick tree branch. Suddenly, a large timber rattlesnake crossed the horse's path. The stallion reared, and Eleanor fell, hitting her head hard on a small boulder. The coroner stated a severe concussion caused her death. Audible gossiping concerning William's bad luck with wives permeated Salem. Was he perchance bewitched? Everyone was aware of his past friendship with Goody Webster, who, after all, died at the end of a rope, convicted by the townspeople of being a witch. A second death during Samhain unnerved the residents. Realizing he might find himself sharing Goody's fate, Will packed up his belongings. As darkness fell, he stealthily left his home to relocate again. This time, he chose Braintree, Massachusetts.

Will set up shop as a cobbler, repairing people's shoes for a modest sum. He married Miss Mary Hall in 1726. They were comfortable together and frequently enjoyed picnics in the bucolic surroundings. Miss Hall, an excellent cook, often included some of Will's favorite foods in the basket lunch.

On October 31, 1762, sitting under a large oak reading poetry together, a sudden storm blew in, pelting them with heavy rains. Scrambling to collect their belongings, neither of them noticed the raven flying for cover nor the blinding streak of lightning until it was too late. Mary's funeral was a few days later.

Will was devastated. He had hoped this wife would grow old with him, but the curse of Samhain was not to be denied. For many years, he didn't dare attempt another relationship. In 1774, with the upheaval in the American colonies, Will worked as a gunsmith. He created muskets for the colonists and didn't even think about getting remarried. He helped pass messages beneath the noses of the British soldiers and was actively engaged in helping the colonists.

One day, a young woman walked into his gun shop with an order for the local militia. Her confidence and beauty were striking. He began courting her, and by year's end, he and Miss Jane Tisdale were married. For the next twenty-seven years, Will and Jane lived harmoniously. They spent many afternoons taking walks in the nearby forests. Will believed he had finally found peace and loved Jane very much.

Jane was an avid gardener. She favored the look of an English garden and spent many years cultivating one. The garden was lined with dahlias, daylilies, and snapdragons, producing a myriad of blooms that lit up the space. A trail of pink roses climbed the white trellis at the yard's entrance, creating a comforting arbor under which Jane loved to read while surveying her handiwork. On the last day of October 1801, while pruning the red roses in the far corner of her property, Jane accidentally stepped near a poisonous arachnid. The venomous spider bit her on her delicate little ankle. Hearing Jane's screams, Will raced to her side. Seeing the creature hiding in the grass next to his beloved wife, Will quickly surmised what had happened. He picked up Jane and raced to the town's doctor. A huge black bird flew behind him as he carried his wife into town. Will was too late. Arriving at the doctor's office, Will saw that Jane was gone.

He returned home in a daze. He collapsed on his knees, weeping bitterly. "This can't be happening again," he moaned. "Goody, my friend, why have you not protected those I love?" There was no response to his pleas, just a rumbling in the sky as thunder and the beginning of Samhain approached.

With Jane's demise, Will decided it was time to move again. People in town were beginning to look askance at him as though he had a third eye or a giant horn growing from his chin. As the night of the bonfires approached, Will packed up his belongings and sneaked off to his next location—Hartford, Connecticut. It was here that he set up a cabinet maker's shop and restarted his life. He mourned Jane, but there was nothing to be done about her untimely death.

After a long period of living by himself, Will began to miss human companionship again. Part of him was afraid of beginning a new relationship, but the solitude was too much to bear. One day, a beautiful young lady entered his store and ordered a dresser for her bedroom. Will couldn't stop staring at her bright violet eyes. Her hair was pitch black, and her skin had a peaches and cream tone that enthralled him. Her name was Miss Katherine Boggs. Will courted her aggressively and eventually won her over. They were married on June 15, 1835, and lived together in Hartford for thirty-eight blissful years. These were the happiest years of Will's life.

Katherine loved the outdoors. She often went hiking with Will, exploring the local forests. On October 31, 1873, Katherine was on one of her usual treks through the forest alone. Will had work to finish in his shop and was to meet her at the bonfire that night. Katherine started her walk a bit later than usual since she wouldn't be meeting Will until dark. Unfortunately, Katherine misjudged the distance she had gone, and when the moon hid behind the clouds, it was difficult to see one foot in front of her. She didn't notice the watchful raven perched on a high branch of a distant tree. Howling sounds and troubling cries were all around her. Katherine sped up the pace of her walk and didn't see a tangled mass of tree roots growing across her path. She stumbled, and all of a sudden, something tore at her right leg. Before she could scream, a pack of wolves descended upon her throat, ripping it out.

It took two days for a search party to find her remains. Will was inconsolable. He fainted at the sight of them, and neighbors put him to bed, where he slept, heavily medicated, for a week. The local doctor and apothecary attended to him. It was a terrible time. Katherine was buried, what was left of her, in a small church cemetery in a private ceremony. Will had nightmares for weeks.

For the next seventeen years, Will lived in Kingston, New York. He had moved again, setting up shop as a blacksmith. He kept to himself, not wanting to risk the closeness of a relationship with another woman. It was just too painful to keep loving and losing. Eventually, love won out, and in 1888, Will met Miss Emily Gray in the Catskill Mountains. Will loved the mountains with their crisp, clean air and solitude. He was taken by surprise when approaching from the opposite direction came a woman who appeared strong and sure-footed. She was birdwatching with a pair of binoculars and didn't notice Will at first, who was quietly reading a book of poetry. Reading was a pastime that didn't require much of his aging body. When she nearly fell over him, she righted herself and provided an introduction.

"Oh, hello," she said. "My name is Emily Gray. I've just been watching that beautiful scarlet tanager over there in the tall oak tree."

"Pleased to meet you," Will replied. "Would you care to share some of my picnic basket provisions?"

"That would be lovely."

From that day on, Will and Miss Gray often went for long walks in the mountains. She taught him about the different species of birds that she could identify, and he showed her how to skip rocks across the streams. Some months later, they decided to marry. The church bells rang on July 12, 1890. Will moved into the new Mrs. Newell's home, and they settled into domestic harmony.

On October 31, 1925, Miss Emily went for a hike in the mountains by herself. She was confident of her way and didn't think twice about climbing to its peak. After about an hour, she felt a strong breeze behind her and tripped, somersaulting over the rocks and the outgrowth. She didn't experience much pain after the first impact. Miss Emily was already comatose as she bounced over the jutting boulders, landing unceremoniously at the bottom of a ravine. At the base of the mountain, she lay with her arms and legs askew and her smashed spectacles a few inches away, a raven circling her body in fascination.

That night, Will called for Goody to visit him. It was his first attempt to contact her after she died in Salem, and he wasn't sure he would be successful. When she appeared after several attempts on his part, he asked her outright, "Why, Goody? Why are my wives dying on Halloween? Why, when I am content and enjoying married life, does it end so tragically?" He wiped a tear from his cheek.

Goody turned away from William and sighed. "There is something I neglected to tell you about the book."

"What do you mean?" William looked intently into her eyes.

"The Rulers of the Universe believe there has to be a ratio of good to evil in the world in order for it to exist. No one and no place is purely one or the other. They created this world with a preponderance of Goodness but included a large measure of Evil as well."

"Go on," said William.

"The book traps the dark forces of this world all year, except for three days during Samhain. At that time, one creature, Morrigan, escapes *The Codex Demonicus* by shapeshifting into a wisp of air. She is then free to set her prophecies of doom in motion. This way, the ratio of Good to Evil in the world is maintained. The prophecies are always fulfilled on Halloween."

"What are you saying, Goody?" asked William incredulously.

"I am saying that the dark forces hate the Keeper of the Book. When Morrigan and her minions are free during Samhain, they punish the Keeper by harming those he loves whenever possible."

"What? Why didn't they punish *you*?" he demanded.

"I have no family, William. There was no one to harm that I cherished. But you had many wives that were dear to you, so they were easy prey."

"Why didn't you tell me this when you gave me the book, Goody?" William spat the words out in anger.

"Because I needed you to take my place. The world needed you. You would have refused if you were aware of the final cost."

"How could you, Goody? Every time I remarried, I sealed another woman's fate!"

"I'm sorry, Will. The forces of Dark Magic were furious that they were trapped in my book. They communicated with Morrigan and her ravens to exact revenge on the Keeper of the book, who, in this case, was you. She foretold the dates of your wives' demise, and her minions carried out the punishments. Your wives died on Halloween because Samhain is the easiest time for the harbingers of doom to pass through to the world of the living and extract their revenge. At that time, Morrigan shapeshifts into a large black bird or raven and sends her minions out to fulfill her missions. I am so sorry to have caused you such pain."

"Take the damned book!" shouted Will. "I don't want it if that's the price for guarding it! I was able to accept my inability to have children, but this is too much!"

"It's too late, Will. I am not corporeal anymore. I cannot possess anything. You agreed to the responsibility, and I'm afraid it's yours for as long as you live," she sighed. He began to protest, but she faded into a smoky, red haze and disappeared from view.

Will searched for a hiding place for the book. After several hours, he located a secret panel behind a wall in his bedroom. Gingerly, Will placed the book inside the panel, obscuring it with a large oak bookcase. Then he sat down on his bed, put his hands over his face, and cried.

Chapter 5

March was milder than most. Maeve and Sylvie were back to pouring over Papa Will's book, sharing the coziness of his worn living room sofa. So far, they had only read about a third of the book, and Maeve was eager to introduce Sylvie to the other mythological creatures.

"Look here." Maeve pointed to an oddly shaped monster with the head of a snake, the hooves of a deer, and a body that was part leopard and part lion.

"Whoa, that is really weird looking."

"That's the Questing Beast," said Maeve, her voice quivering with excitement. "I think he's the most fascinating of all the monsters in this book. He's the only one made up of several creatures combined, and he's immortal," she added. "He's also the one that visits my dreams."

"He gives me the creeps." A shiver ran through Sylvie's body. "Let's close the book and do something else."

Maeve found blank writing paper and a few pens and pencils in one of Papa Will's desk drawers. The two girls played several games of Hangman before Maeve noticed it was getting darker outside.

"I think we should go now," Maeve suggested. "It's getting late, and I have to walk Pooch before I make supper for my dad."

Sylvie agreed. The girls left Papa Will's and headed off together before separating as they approached the woods. Maeve reminded Sylvie to go around the woods, "just so you don't get lost or meet any hungry animals!"

Maeve watched Sylvie disappear around the path. She headed home at a quickened pace as the sun went down in the sky.

That night, Sylvie woke with a start. Her heart was pounding, and she could barely catch her breath. Her body was shaking, and her limbs felt so heavy she could barely move them. She checked the corners of her room, dreading what she might find. There was nothing there.

As her breath slowed, Sylvie remembered her dream. She was being chased by the Questing Beast hissing behind her, its hooves hammering the floor of the forest. The beast—spotted like a leopard—was accompanied by the cries of what sounded like a pack of wild animals snarling behind her. A glance over her left shoulder caused her stomach to knot, and the spittle dripping from the creature's jaws repulsed her. She could smell the beast's foul breath as it encircled her, when she was jolted awake by the sound of her father's television, the volume turned up too high. She sighed with relief. *I guess I need to lay off reading that book of Maeve's for a while. That dream was too real.* She walked to the bathroom, washed her face with cold water, and turned on her lamp.

Sylvie tried to read one of her favorite books of poetry, but she just couldn't get rid of the awful images and noises in her mind. She left her lamp on and tried to go back to sleep, but her eyes remained open in a state of alertness until it was time to rise for school.

The next week, a package arrived for Sylvie. The return address was her Grandmother Amelia's. Sylvie hoped it would be a birthday present for her sixteenth birthday on March 15th. The kids in her previous school teased her mercilessly when they studied Shakespeare's *Julius Caesar* and learned that "The Ides of March" was a bad luck day. It was, after all, the day the Romans assassinated Caesar, and it was tough for Sylvie to live down. The fact that she was a shy girl made her an easy target, and she dreaded her birthday every year. That was the main reason she had not shared the information with anyone in Wren Falls—not even Maeve.

The other secret Sylvie kept was her artistic ability. She was a gifted painter, but hated people evaluating her work. It was her private world—the world of her art—and she kept it to herself. It was a sort of delicious feeling, knowing something about yourself that your peers didn't know about you. Only her father and Nana Amelia were aware of her artistic abilities and interest.

Sylvie took the package in and placed it on the desk in her bedroom. She carefully unwrapped the colorful paper protecting what was inside. As she gingerly pulled it away, she was rewarded with the sight of a complete set of Daniel Smith Extra Fine Watercolors and several new round brushes in different sizes. She squealed with delight when she noticed the addition of new colors like Pyrrole Crimson and Moonglow and was thrilled to get more Neutral Tint, which was always running low. Sylvie finally got around to reading her grandmother's note:

March 14th

Dearest Sylvie,

I miss you and your dad so much. I hope you are happy in your new home and are making new friends. These paints and brushes are my way of letting you know that I remember everything about you and think of you often. Happy Birthday, my beloved granddaughter.

Love,

Nana Amelia

Sylvie wiped a tear from her eye and set about writing a thank-you note to Nana. This habit was a holdover from her mother, Karen, who always impressed upon her the necessity for a personal note of thanks—a small memory of her mom that she carried in her heart. Always.

The next day, she went off to school in a cheerful mood, meeting up with Maeve on the way there.

"Wanna go to the Historical Society and check out some more creepy articles and unsolved crimes?" Maeve asked her.

"Maybe tomorrow," Sylvie answered. "I've got stuff to do today." She was celebrating her birthday with her dad, whose long work hours kept them from spending as much time together as they would have liked. He made an exception for her birthday, and she was looking forward to it.

In the evening, Sylvie and her dad shared her father's chocolate fudge brownies, straight out of a Betty Crocker mix, with vanilla frosting from a Betty Crocker tub. It was the only thing he baked, and it was a special treat for his daughter's birthday. He had placed sixteen candles on the brownies and added one more for good luck. In his off-key voice, he sang "Happy Birthday" to her. Afterwards, he gave her a card with $16 and kissed her on the forehead. Sylvie noted the absence of her mother and brother without comment, but the pain was softened by the love Sylvie and her father shared. It was a beautiful night, and all was, for the moment, right with the world. Sylvie went to bed content and relaxed, thinking about the pictures she would create with Nana Amelia's painting supplies.

Sylvie was running for her life. Breathless, sweat poured down her face, her arms, her legs. Her mouth was drier than the desert in a sandstorm. The cries of wild dogs mingled with the sounds of hooves scraping the ground behind her. She quickly glanced over her right shoulder. Whatever was chasing her would soon be upon her. The hissing got louder, the growling more insistent. Suddenly, she cried out in pain as the creature tore at her shirt with its sharp, pointed fangs! Sylvie ran full out with the little energy she had left. She just had enough time to grab the doorknob, rush inside, and bolt the door as the beast smashed into it! The monster righted itself and Sylvie caught a horrifying glimpse of it pounding on the old wooden door with its hooves. After roaring loudly, it gave up and ran toward the forest, searching for easier prey. Sylvie saw the shadow of its misshapen form lumbering between the great oaks as its cries dissipated.

Leaning against the door, straining to catch her breath, Sylvie was sure this was not a dream. The horror of her experience washed over her. *What was that thing? Where did it come from? Why was it chasing me? Was this the same creature that had invaded Maeve's and my dreams?*

As her breath slowed and her legs regained their strength, Sylvie walked slowly into the kitchen and drank a large glass of orange juice. Her energy restored, she went into her bedroom. She turned to look at her back in her three-way mirror and noticed a long red scratch down the center of her torso. Repulsed, she jumped in the shower and just stood under the hot spray for two hours washing herself over and over again.

Sometime later, when she calmed down, she pulled out her watercolors and new brushes, taking some paper out of her bottom dresser drawer. After a momentary pause, Sylvie began to put her impressions of the creature onto paper. The process frightened her. The image was so life-like that she had to put the painting away in her closet. *Maybe I'll be able to work on it during the day. The sunlight will keep me focused, and I won't give in to my fears* she promised herself. She pulled the artwork out of the closet, and placed it in the corner of her room to be worked on tomorrow. Sylvie shuddered as she looked at it. A chill crept down her back, and she was reminded of the long red scratch that divided her torso and the horrifying creature that put it there. *Where did the vicious beast come from? I wonder if anyone else in Wren Falls has seen it.*

The next day, Sylvie and Maeve shared their sandwiches at lunch beneath their favorite tree. "What did you do yesterday?" asked Maeve.

"Nothin' much. Just sorted through some old family photos with my dad. I promised him I'd help him put them in an album in some kind of order. It was important to him since my brother, Charlie, and Mom are gone."

Maeve recalled the loss of her own mother. She carried an old picture of Alice in her purse that she had found in a trunk in her parents' bedroom. Looking at it from time to time was the only way she could remember her mother's face. Passing time had a way of erasing that memory, and Maeve was grateful for the snapshot, worn as it was. "That must have been tough." Maeve put her arm around Sylvie to comfort her.

Sylvie smiled at her friend. "Yeah. We better get inside. Lunch is just about over, and we don't want to get detention from Miss Clouder for being late."

Maeve nodded, and both girls quickly cleaned up their trash and ran into the building. They had agreed to meet after school at the Historical Society. Maeve was keen on checking out the cold cases—the unsolved cases that had puzzled the small Wren Falls police department for years. Sylvie usually found this research fascinating, but she was unusually quiet this afternoon.

"What's wrong?" Maeve asked.

"Oh, nothin'."

"I guess you're still thinkin' about that album you put together yesterday, huh?"

Sylvie didn't answer at first. She wasn't sure she should tell Maeve what happened yesterday. Maeve might think she was crazy. She was her only friend in town, and didn't want to push her away. After a while, Sylvie decided she had to share the frightening experience with someone she trusted, or she *would* go crazy. So, she began, slowly, to recount the events of the previous afternoon.

"You have to promise not to tell anyone what I'm going to tell you," Sylvie said in a stern tone.

"Okay, okay, I swear." Maeve was getting a bit agitated. She paced nervously. "What *is* it?

Sylvie began to recount the events of the previous afternoon. After every few sentences, she paused, allowing the details to sink in. Maeve went from pale to alabaster until she was the color of Sylvie's bright white watercolor paper. *I should never have told her.* Sylvie regretted her admission.

"Go on," Maeve insisted. "Finish your story." By the time Sylvie had finished, she was shaking.

"Well?" Sylvie stared at Maeve. "Say something," she insisted.

For several moments, Maeve said nothing. She didn't know how to tell Sylvie that she had experienced much the same thing. She hadn't told Sylvie for fear that Sylvie would never believe her, and that would be the end of their friendship. Not sharing her secret had put Sylvie in danger. Would she be able to forgive Maeve for that?

Sylvie turned to Maeve. "I should never have told you. I've ruined everything." She got up to leave.

"Wait!" Maeve called after her. "I believe you. I do. I had the same thing happen to me, but I didn't have the nerve to tell you."

Sylvie turned to Maeve, her jaw hanging open and her eyes wide circles in her pale face. "What? How could you not tell me?"

"I thought you'd think less of me—that I was out of my mind," said Maeve. "Please, come back here, and let's talk."

Sylvie hesitated, but in the end, she valued Maeve's friendship and decided to listen to her friend's story. They exited the Historical Society and sat down on the backsteps for some much-needed privacy.

Maeve began to recount her experience with Pooch, the day the creature came after them. Although Maeve had not had a good look at the monster, the cries and growls frightened her. She quickened her pace as the hissing, and the hooves behind her came closer. When she was done describing the incident, there was silence.

"If this is true, it's really scary," Sylvie shuddered.

"It *is* true. I *swear* it," replied Maeve. "I think we need to check Papa Will's book again. I'm pretty sure this creature is the Questing Beast, come to life! If I'm right, this town is in real trouble. Don't tell anyone our secret. Let's meet at my grandpa's place the day after tomorrow and *stay out of the woods!*"

"*Deal!*" Sylvie shook her head emphatically.

They hurried home, looking over their shoulders, anxious to avoid any confrontation with the frightening creature. Both girls were now sure that the creature was real and not a figment of their imaginations. They were also aware that the people of Wren Falls were in serious danger.

Chapter 6

Sylvie and Maeve clambered up the creaky front steps of Papa Will's home. They ran upstairs to collect the book, still stashed under the stack of old photos. Maeve eagerly grabbed her seat on the old sofa. Sylvie approached the book with much trepidation. She wasn't all that anxious to see the creature close up. Unbeknownst to Maeve and Sylvie's dad, Sylvie had started to paint her impressions of the creature that was chasing them. She stopped when she was halfway done because the image frightened her and caused her to relive the terrifying incident.

They had leafed through about half of the book when it fell to the floor, open to the inside of the front cover. Maeve recognized her grandfather's distinctive penmanship. In fine print were the words, "This encyclopedia details the ancient creatures that the Celts believed were responsible for all the evils that walked the earth. There is no evidence that survived the millennia to prove those creatures' existence."

Below the disclaimer was a chart. It was entitled *Marriage Record*, and a quick survey of the document revealed that it was a listing of Papa Will's marriages:

Marriage Record

Bride's Name	Marriage Date	Groom's Name
Megan O'Brien b. January 3, 1645 d. October 31, 1689	June 6, 1669	William Makepeace Newell b. December 12, 1640 d.
Abigail Williams b. June 17, 1670 d. October 31, 1710	August 14, 1701	William Makepeace Newell b. December 12, 1640 d.
Eleanor Briggs b. May 7, 1682 d. October 31, 1722	November 7, 1715	William Makepeace Newel b. December 12, 1640 d.
Mary Hall b. April 15, 1708 d. October 31, 1762	March 2, 1726	William Makepeace Newell b. December 12, 1640 d.
Jane Tisdale b. May 1, 1754 d. October 31, 1801	July 22, 1774	William Makepeace Newell b. December 12, 1640 d.
Katherine Boggs b. March 7, 1817 d. October 31, 1873	June 15, 1835	William Makepeace Newell b. December 12, 1640 d.
Emily Gray b. September 4, 1850 d. October 31, 1925	July 12, 1890	William Makepeace Newell b. December 12, 1640 d.
Elizabeth Hathaway b. April 17, 1950 d. October 31, 1973	May 16, 1971	William Makepeace Newell b. December 12, 1640 d. October 31, 2006

"Oh, my gosh!" squeaked Sylvie. "How many times was your grandfather married, Maeve?"

"I have no idea. I assumed it was just once!"

The girls noticed other puzzling anomalies.

"Look, Maeve. Each wife died on October 31st!"

"Yeah," Maeve spoke slowly. "And look at the date of his first marriage to Megan O'Brien. It was on June 6, 1669. Papa Will's date of death was October 31, 2006. That would make him over three hundred years old when he died! I wonder who entered his date of death on this chart?"

Sylvie shivered. "This is too weird! Why did they all die on Halloween?"

"I don't know." Maeve scratched her head, deep in thought. "But I'm going to get to the bottom of this mystery. Let's put the book away."

Sylvie was only too happy to oblige. She and Maeve replaced the book in the attic and said their goodbyes. They headed for their respective houses, taking the long way home to avoid the woods.

"What is *this*?" Sylvie's father demanded. She had just walked through the front door when he approached her with his hands holding several half-finished paintings of her nemesis.

"Why were you in my room, Dad?"

"I was looking for the field trip form you asked me to sign, and I found these horrific paintings on your desk. They're a far cry from the lovely landscapes and portraits you usually create. They are gruesome, Sylvie. What's going on?" His face was flushed, and his eyes bulged under scowling brows.

Thinking fast, Sylvie said, "Nothing's going on, Dad. There's a contest at school to find the most imaginative creation in any medium. I decided to try for the prize. It's a hundred dollar gift card to the art supply store in the next town over, Pinckney Gorge. I'm always running out of supplies."

"Well, if that's all this is, I guess I can understand your participation, but you had me really worried, honey."

"Don't be silly, Dad. What else could it be?" She smiled, took the pictures from him, and walked calmly into her room. She closed the door, leaned against it, and exhaled, hoping he wouldn't hear her heart pounding in her chest as she shoved the paintings into her closet.

Maeve was having no such problem with her father. He was passed out drunk when she arrived home. *Honestly, I don't know how his body can absorb all that alcohol and keep going strong. It's a wonder he can survive on so little real food.* Sometimes it was a relief, though. She was rarely accountable to him for anything, and there were few rules she had to follow at home.

Still, there were times when she wished she had a father like Sylvie's, a dad who cared deeply for his daughter and showed it. *Oh, well,* she said to herself, *maybe someday I'll do something that will make him really notice me, and he'll finally be grateful he has a daughter.*

Maeve walked over to her bedroom window and stared at the stars in the sky. It was a beautiful night, and stargazing was one of her favorite activities. At least it always was, until this night, when she suddenly noticed a giant snake with protruding red eyes staring right back at her from the other side of the glass as it hung from the nearest branch of her favorite tree. Her scream brought her father running in his awkward, lopsided way to her room, half drunk, as he began coming out of his stupor.

"Oh, my God, Maeve! What is it?" he managed to get out.

Maeve pointed to the window. "There! A huge snake! Hissing at me!"

Her father looked out the window in all directions, but found nothing. He gave his daughter a rare hug.

"There, there, Maeve. Don't worry. I have those bad visions, too, especially when I've mixed my whiskey with rum. You'll be okay. Just get ready for bed. A good night's sleep will do you good." He left Maeve to her thoughts in the empty room, which did not provide the necessary ingredients for a peaceful night's sleep.

Chapter 7

After Miss Gray's unfortunate demise, William swore off any further romantic entanglements. He had done this before, but this time, he was aware that age was catching up to him. William noticed the changes on his insides even as his outer appearance aged more slowly. Will looked older than he did when he got the book from Goody, but not much older, and he couldn't endure any more loss. He really considered married life to be a thing of the past for him until he met Elizabeth Hathaway in the year 1970.

William had relocated to Wren Falls, New York, to work a small farm in semi-retirement. On a trip into the tiny town to sell his eggs to the grocer, he met Elizabeth Hathaway at the counter, purchasing some fabric with which to make a new dress. "That's a lovely color, Miss. It matches your eyes perfectly," said William, always enchanted by a pretty face. Miss Elizabeth was only twenty years young, possessed of a trim but curvaceous figure, striking auburn hair, and light blue eyes. That day, a friendship between the two of them began and eventually developed into a more intimate relationship. By then, William was over three hundred years old but didn't look a day over forty-five. The relationship led to marriage in May 1971, although William had foresworn such a commitment in the past.

If anyone stopped William in the street and asked him how his honeymoon period was going, he would describe it as "idyllic." He was completely besotted with his new bride and gave her whatever she craved. She had a definite comfort level with livestock, and her ability to produce healthy, beautiful horses was magical. William built a large stable on his land and filled it with various equine specimens, including imported horses from other countries.

After about a year, Elizabeth remarked that a new neighbor had moved in a mile down the road from their farm. She told William that she bumped into him while buying supplies for her animals. She mentioned that the neighbor was very interested in her horses and wanted to develop his own stables with Arabian horses. The new neighbor, Miles McKay, had invited her to visit his farm and give him some tips on the proper care of these sensitive creatures.

"Go ahead, visit," Will encouraged her. "You'll be a big help to him, I'm sure."

Will was quite proud of his wife's acumen and trusted her completely. So, Elizabeth began to make weekly visits to the McKay farm. She spent an hour or so there, instructing Miles McKay in the secrets of successfully developing his herd. In the beginning, they were just good neighbors. Over time, the relationship grew more intense. Elizabeth and Miles became lovers.

After about four months of intimacy, Elizabeth became pregnant. She told Miles about the pregnancy, but he admitted he was not ready to have children. When she began to show, Elizabeth understood that she would have to tell Will, and she dreaded the confrontation. When another three weeks had passed, Will, seeing her figure changing, commented, "Farm life suits you, my dear. You appear to be filling out and curvier," he said with a sly grin. Elizabeth took advantage of Will's mood and lured him into the bedroom. After a passionate interlude, she spoke to him in her sultry voice.

"Will, darling, I have a surprise for you."

"What more could I ask of you after the hour we just spent together?" he smiled.

"Will, I'm with child," Elizabeth whispered.

"But that's impossible," Will replied. "As I told you before, I can't have children. I never have with any of my earlier wives."

"Miracles do happen, Will, especially with a love as powerful as ours. Be happy, darling."

Will said no more. He thought about it for the next few weeks and decided it was possible that a girl as young and fertile as his wife might be able to overcome the witch's prophecy. He was happy about the news and decided to just accept it gratefully.

Some months later, Elizabeth gave birth to a healthy boy. She called him James Makepeace Newell, and Will was thrilled. He grew very attached to his son, and when the boy was old enough to walk, Will took him to meet the animals and view the gardens. He was the joy of Will's life, besides Elizabeth.

One night, Goody Webster appeared in Will's dream. She held out her left arm and pointed her index finger at Will. "Goody," Will cried out. "You were wrong about my lack of children. Look at my beautiful son in the next room!" He was overcome with happiness.

Goody looked at him with a sad expression on her face and said simply, "All is not what it appears to be," and with that, she slowly disappeared.

"Come back, Goody," Will beseeched her. "What do you mean?"

In a fading voice, she said to him, "In time, Will…"

Several days later, Miles McKay came to visit Elizabeth, ostensibly to ask for some advice with his breathtaking Arabians. In actuality, Miles had resolved to break off his relationship with Elizabeth and told her so. He wanted nothing to do with the baby. It was a painful breakup since he was still infatuated with her.

It was the first meeting between Will and Miles. Will was struck by the physical resemblance between Miles McKay and his son, James Newell. The matching clefts in their chins and the deep dimples in their cheeks were obvious. The lingering gaze that Miles cast on Elizabeth, as he took his leave, was infuriating. It was all Will could do to contain himself until Miles went home to his own farm.

When Miles was gone and James Newell was down for a nap, Will confronted Elizabeth, demanding the truth about her relationship with Miles. She begged him to leave her alone, said he'd wake the little boy, of course, the boy was Will's, etc. Finally, she broke down amidst a rush of tears and admitted that the boy was Miles's. She hoped he would accept the boy as his son.

Will was enraged. His wife's betrayal was like a shot in the stomach. He had given her everything. "You whore!" He hurled the ugly words in her face. "How could you?" he screamed at her and ran out of the house into the woods surrounding their home.

Elizabeth was frightened by the intensity of Will's anger. He was in a rage, something that she had never seen before. Will had always been loving and cheerful with her. This was a Will she did not recognize. She hoped the anger would pass and that they would reconcile. She was certain that Miles would never be interested in raising his own child, and she hoped, desperately, that Will would forgive her with the passage of time. Little did she know what Will had in store for her.

Elizabeth's massive deception reached a very dark place in Will's heart. His rage turned cold as he thought night and day about avenging his wife's betrayal. He stopped talking to Elizabeth and spent less time with his son, even though he still loved him. He spent hours planning his revenge and finally reached out to Goody Webster for help. He prayed every night for her to reappear, and finally, on October 29, 1973, he was able to reach her.

He described his plight and his desire to punish Elizabeth. He asked Goody for advice, and she sadly replied, "Leave the child alone. He is an innocent. Be very sure of your decision, for there is no turning back once you have started the ritual. I beg you to reconsider." But Will was insistent.

"You owe me, Goody. I guarded your book in good faith, and you deceived me. Not only am I unable to sire any offspring, but for over two centuries, my beloved wives were also sacrificed. The cost was too dear."

Again, Goody tried to change his mind, but there was no dissuading Will. She eventually gave in to his demands.

"Go to the book, *The Codex Demonicus,* and look at the inside of the back cover. There is a flap on the cover. Hidden inside it are incantations for calling up all of the creatures in the book. Pick one of these incantations to bring forth the evil being you choose to exact your revenge."

William continued to bombard her with questions.

"When should I do this? What do I do with James during this time? Surely, he will hear her screams?"

Goody Webster sighed deeply, realizing there was no stopping Will's plan. "You will do this on October 31st, during Samhain. After Elizabeth is asleep, I will bind your son with a spell that will move both of you to the bonfire, away from the sounds and sights of this ghastly event. After the deed is done, I will make sure that James is again asleep and there is nothing to implicate you in Elizabeth's death. I will return you and your sleeping child to your home. You will put James to bed, and then you will scream for help at the top of your lungs!

"The mortician will remove Elizabeth's remains. The townspeople will believe that an ancient monster was released during Samhain and, unfortunately for your family, attacked Elizabeth in her sleep while you were at the bonfire with your boy. When you return home, you will 'learn' of the awful murder of your dear wife. You will never reveal to your son what actually took place. He will think his mother died in her sleep. He is too young to absorb the real details from the good inhabitants of Wren Falls. They will all be too traumatized to discuss the crime, anyway."

"This is truly a diabolical plan," Will grinned, his eyes shining. "Thank you, Goody. I shall follow your instructions to the letter."

A great weight lifted off Will's chest as it positioned itself on Goody's. She would regret her part in this play forever. Will had helped her in her hour of need, and she was obliged to do the same for him. As for Will, he couldn't wait until the 31st, unaware that he had changed at his core, having taken up residence in the Devil's Lair.

How had everything gone so wrong? I have loved Elizabeth deeply since the first day I met her. I gave her everything she desired, yet she has betrayed me with another lover.

The rage bubbled inside him, needing an outlet. *It is true what they say. Love and Hate are two sides of the same coin. It is an easy transition from Love to Hate. All you need is the right catalyst and adultery definitely fit the bill.*

Will-needed revenge, which fueled his motivation to destroy Elizabeth. He could barely contain his emotions as he put his devious plan into motion. It was especially difficult when Will was around his wife. He couldn't wait for the deed to be done.

At the same time, he was more attached to James than ever before. The older the boy got, the more activities they were able to do together. The bond between them was extremely strong.

He hoped James would not be permanently scarred by the death of his mother.

Will had disappointed Goody and put her in a difficult position. He cared for her, but he believed she was in his debt. He couldn't worry about her feelings now. He had to get on with his mission and eliminate his cheating wife.

It was Halloween 1973, and Will was energized by the task before him. His hatred of Elizabeth had only grown more intense, and he was eager to be rid of her. Conversely, his love for James Newell had only grown stronger. The two emotions were at war within him, and he was anxious to simplify his life.

As the sun was setting, Will prepared a sleeping draught for his wife. He gave it to her under the pretext of caring deeply about her well-being. The two were now talking again, and Will pretended to be over his pique. Noting that she had seemed tired recently, he beseeched her to drink it all and get a good night's sleep. He told her he would take care of little James, and she could sleep carefree. He had everything set for the evening.

In the next room, James was watching TV. William went down the cellar steps and went to a corner of the dark room where he had already lit a dozen candles. The week before, Will had studied the incantations on the back of *The Codex Demonicus* and selected the one that would bring forth the Questing Beast, believing that it would satisfy his thirst for blood. He put on a black robe that Goody had given him and began his incantation:

Nomine Demonicus voyis ayudan
Revanicle mewyzicor dormiculus
Questoribin Anigamicus

He repeated it six times, and after the sixth time, Goody Webster appeared, holding a sleeping James in her arms. She handed him to Will and cast her spell. The boy and his father were suddenly transported to the bonfire watching the flames with rapt attention. There was some commotion coming from the direction of Will's home. The Samhain celebrants were oblivious as they stared intently at the bonfire. At the end of the ceremony, Will carried his son, who was finally asleep, home to his little bed. William noticed a fat raven perched on the roof of his house. Goody had cast a sleeping spell upon the boy that would not end until the following day. When William entered the house, he was taken aback. The rooms had been ransacked, all the furniture was upended, and a rotten stench permeated the residence.

The bedroom held Elizabeth's remains, which were barely recognizable. Will ran from his home, yelling for help, and his neighbors soon came running. The mortician removed the remains, and women from the town came with buckets, mops, and rags to clean up the mess left behind. At about 3 a.m., Will fell asleep on his couch.

The townspeople buried Elizabeth Newell the next day in the churchyard cemetery. Will, surrounded by an abundance of sympathetic neighbors, cried copious amounts of crocodile tears. He thanked them for their support and put his farm and home up for sale, saying the memories of Elizabeth's death made living there too painful. Thereafter, Will moved with James to the little cottage that remained his abode for the rest of his life. He hid *The Codex Demonicus* in the secret panel behind the bookcase in his bedroom, where it remained for the rest of his "unnatural" life.

Chapter 8

April arrived. Crocuses peeked out from the ground, and ornamental cherry trees began to unfurl their lovely pink blossoms. Sylvie and Maeve took advantage of the beautiful signs of spring to take a walk through the town. "Let's stop by the Historical Society, Maeve, and continue our research. It's so beautiful outside. I don't think anything can bring me down!"

"Okay," said Maeve. "We have so many mysteries to solve, and we've been away from it for a while. It'll be good to get back to our research." They stopped at the laundry, went up the creaky wooden stairs, and entered the Society's rooms, which were pretty empty. "I guess most people are outside enjoying the change in the weather."

"That's fine. It'll be quieter and easier for us to concentrate."

The first thing they looked through was a machine that showed old newspaper articles from the Wren Falls Gazette. The paper had a crime section in each issue, and the girls hungrily poured over the headlines.

"Look at this one!" Maeve ran over to Sylvie with the newspaper. She read, "Death of Miss Elizabeth Hathaway Unsolved".

Reading on, the girls learned that Miss Hathaway died violently on October 31, 1973, and no suspect had been found. The case was still unsolved.

Maeve read the article out loud. "Witnesses proved unreliable: one swore a low growl, like that of a leopard, was followed by the screams of Miss Hathaway. Another added he was startled by what sounded like a giant snake hissing loudly at the time. A third mentioned the sound of hooves pounding on the ground just as Miss Hathaway yelled for help. The police were frustrated, and there was little left of Miss Hathaway to do any forensic analysis."

The girls looked at each other with their eyes opened wide.

Maeve continued reading, "Miss Hathaway's married name was Mrs. Elizabeth Newell, wife of William Makepeace Newell." An audible gasp came from Maeve and Sylvie simultaneously.

The girls clumsily grabbed their materials and hurried out of the library. They walked home in silence. Maeve was in a daze. When they got to the fork in the road where their paths diverged, Sylvie asked simply, "Are you all right, Maeve?"

Maeve nodded. She still hadn't spoken a word. It was as if she was spellbound.

"Maybe I should walk you home," Sylvie offered. I'm worried about you.

Call me when you get home," Sylvie whispered.

Maeve shook her head no to Sylvie's suggestion to walk Maeve home. She barely got out "Okay" to the requested phone call and turned in the direction of her home.

Sylvie watched her for a few minutes until she was out of sight. Then she ran home like her life depended on it, not stopping until she reached her front door.

Maeve walked with the jerky movements of a marionette and arrived at her front door, still in a trance. Trying to digest what she had learned, she was oblivious to the menacing growl that followed her. It was Pooch's loud barking, as he waited faithfully on her front steps, that jolted Maeve out of her trance—just before the creature pounced.

The creature slammed into Maeve's front door, inches away from the terrified girl. It bounced off the door with such force that it landed several feet away, just allowing Maeve the seconds she needed to open the damaged door, hurry into the house with Pooch, and lock it. She pushed the living room club chair against the door and prayed that the monster would give up and leave. It was still daylight, and this was no shadow. The fact that it was getting bolder made her shivering more pronounced, and her legs assumed the structure of JELL-O.

After about an hour, Maeve got up the nerve to peek out the living room curtains and noticed that the creature had left. She fell, crumpled, into the club chair as her mind raced with a million questions. *What had caused Elizabeth Newell's death? Why hadn't her grandfather ever mentioned the circumstances of Elizabeth's death to Maeve? Why had he married so many times? What was the significance of October 31st?*

The pain in Maeve's head, that began just behind her eyes, threatened to split her head open. It spread down her neck and into her shoulders, burning like an out-of-control fire. She awkwardly rose from the chair and staggered into her bedroom, where she collapsed onto her bed. Maeve fought sleep and the horrifying dreams that often accompanied it for as long as she could until fatigue overtook her. She tossed and turned throughout the night.

Another nightmare held her hostage. The evil creature was banging on the front door, pawing it in a fury. Growls, roars, hisses, and cries surrounded the house. Maeve was screaming for help, but no one came. The dream was even worse than before because when she opened her door, there were claw marks on it, and Pooch was lying on the front steps, mortally wounded. She cried loudly during the dream, and her wracking sobs woke her. Maeve was exhausted and got up to check that Pooch was all right. She was relieved to find him peacefully sleeping under the kitchen table. Sometime later, she was vaguely aware of her father stumbling into the little house and prayed he was alone.

Chapter 9

Alice Carr, Maeve's mother, was a local farmer's niece when she met James Newell at a September Harvest Dance in town. She was immediately smitten with his natural good looks and charm. He stood over six feet tall with jet-black hair, clear blue eyes, and a trim physique. The attraction was mutual, and the two began dating shortly thereafter.

Alice had a particular talent for raising fruits, vegetables, and exotic flowers on her uncle's farm. She designed floral bouquets that she sold to customers in several nearby towns, not just in Wren Falls. Her reputation as a creative florist was spreading throughout the community.

James, raised on his papa's farm, had become quite knowledgeable about animal husbandry. He had a knack for calming and training his horses, in addition to maximizing the number of other animals that he raised for profit. His egg business was now triple the size that it had been under his father's supervision. James was also very handy at carpentry and masonry.

He helped his father build their original home and, in the future, would build a home for Alice and any children they might have.

When James finally proposed to Alice, she excitedly agreed to the marriage and ran into town the next day to meet with the town's singular dressmaker, Nelda Harrison. Alice wanted a wedding dress that would be simple yet elegant. At her first meeting with Nelda, the women established a strong rapport. This connection continued until the untimely death of Alice Newell, recorded as Unsolved Case #666 in the local police files.

Nelda Harrison and Alice Newell became fast friends. They visited each other often, sharing a coffee and Alice's latest confection. Sometimes, they met at the farm and other times in Nelda's shop during her lunch break. They were as close as sisters, and as Maeve grew up, she came to call Nelda "Aunt Nelda," having no other aunts, uncles, or siblings to confide in. It was to Aunt Nelda that Maeve went for comfort after Alice's cruel death. For the next several years, Nelda visited Maeve once a month just to be sure she was okay—to read her stories, and make her a home-cooked meal.

James, always fond of his liquor, had gone off the deep end after Alice's death. He let his appearance go, not bathing or brushing his hair, dressing carelessly, and cutting himself off from his friends and customers. He was often in his own world, talking to his dead wife and ignoring his young daughter. His only occupation seemed to be running the still in the woods and sampling its product. Occasionally, a neighbor would purchase some of his whiskey, but most of it he kept for himself. There was little food in the house, and Maeve was frequently hungry. Her father often took his meals at the local bar, where the owner let him run a tab. The grocer let Maeve run a tab, up to a point, and that, plus Nelda's contributions, were all that kept her from starving.

Alice and James's early days of their marriage were idyllic. James tended to his animals, and Alice to her gardening and horticulture. Their union produced a sole daughter, Maeve. Alice became a proficient baker and a creative homemaker. James was respected by the men in the community. Locals often came to him for advice concerning their livestock or help in constructing a neighbor's home. Will was proud of his son and admired his daughter-in-law. He often stopped by to visit and share a whiskey with James.

Until—James took up drinking as a pastime. He became bored with the life of a country gentleman. James began to frequent Flannery's Bar & Grill in town, arriving home later and later. He constructed his own rudimentary still in the woods and spent more time away from his family. James missed meals, time with his daughter, and time in bed with his wife.

In the meantime, Alice met a young farmer, Collum Carmichael, from the next town over. She developed the habit of chatting with him about gardens and greenhouses on her weekly trips to Wren Falls to replenish gardening supplies. After making their purchases, the two would walk over to a small café in town for tea and conversation. The conversation was lively and filled the void left by her absent husband. There was a mutual attraction that began to blossom between the two gardeners, and Alice found herself looking forward to their weekly rendezvous. She shared her feelings with Nelda, who listened but did not advise. Poor Alice's emotions ran in all directions. She wanted to remain loyal to her husband, but his abandonment had led her to seek solace elsewhere. She was very attracted to Collum, who, she discovered, was her distant cousin. They bore a family resemblance, which amused them both.

After many weeks of seeing each other, Alice and Collum decided to picnic under her favorite old oak tree. One thing led to another, and Collum leaned in for a passionate kiss. Unbeknownst to either of them, Alice's father-in-law was coming up the path. He spied them in a heated embrace. The rage boiled up in him, blinding him to any rational thought. He hid behind a nearby tree and recalled his own wife's adultery with Miles McKay so many years before.

And he recalled the way he terminated it.

Will started to make plans for revenge against Alice. He went down to the cellar and sought out his robe, candles, and the incantation that had roused the Questing Beast against Elizabeth. The monster had made short work of her, and Will was sure that it would be equally effective against Alice. Will hated disloyalty, and what he had seen between Alice and Collum took him to the darkest place in his being. He didn't think of how this decision would affect his son or his granddaughter. He was blinded by his hatred of the two lovers. His ire pushed him to move quickly, with a new-found energy that propelled him to complete his plan. He couldn't wait to bring it to fruition.

Chapter 10

May passed in a blur. It was mercifully uneventful, and the girls were looking forward to spending the summer together. An overnight in the mountains was to be the culminating activity of the year for their class, and Miss Clouder would be the chaperone for the group of students. Maeve and Sylvie felt safe in the mountains since the creature appeared to live primarily in the woods and the surrounding environments. There were only seven students in the upper class, ranging from eleven to sixteen, and the six oldest were planning to go on the field trip. As the date of the weekend approached, excitement built. Few of the students could concentrate on their end-of-year studies. Sylvie and Maeve handed their signed permission slips to Ms. Clouder and resolved to enjoy their little excursion.

The weekend of June 24th loomed large in their imaginations. The group was to leave Wren Falls on a school bus on Saturday morning. They would arrive at Faith's Crossing, a small town at the foot of the mountains, in two hours. Miss Clouder had arranged for a cold breakfast they could eat on the bus to save time. Maeve would have liked to explore the little town for a while, but that was not on the itinerary.

When everyone had finished eating, they all put their trash in a large plastic bag and dropped it in a trash container in town. Miss Clouder was very strict about cleaning up one's garbage and stressed the need to take care of the environment, as she often did at school. Next, the students, attired in bright green t-shirts with "Wren Falls" written on them, started their five-mile hike up the mountain. Sylvie and Maeve exchanged glances and secretly hoped that this would be a great weekend with no drama. After about an hour, Miss Clouder found an acceptable location for a campsite.

"This looks like the perfect place to camp," observed the teacher. "It's a large enough clearing with a lovely lake just around the bend. People, pull out your tents, and let's get them set up." The class worked for a while, helping each other set up the campsite, collecting wood for a fire, and putting mosquito netting over the tents.

"Time for lunch," said Miss Clouder. She opened the cooler she had brought with her and began to hand out sandwiches and chips to everyone.

"She really is so organized!" Sylvie whispered to Maeve.

"So far, so good." Maeve smiled.

After lunch, the group grabbed the fishing poles they brought with them that were stored in the underbelly of the bus. They carried the poles along with their knapsacks during the hike and were finally going to use them. Each student brought a water bottle along with the pole and spent a few minutes digging with their hands in the ground, looking for worms to use as bait. Living in Wren Falls, most of them had fished before in the brooks, streams, rivers, and lakes that were omnipresent in the mountains. They filed out in a double line and walked to the lake. Everyone dropped their lines into the water and waited for telltale movement. The lake apparently was well stocked because by late afternoon, everybody had caught at least one trout, and the campers returned to the campsite, eager to have the fish for dinner.

Miss Clouder showed the students how to clean the fish, and then they set to cleaning and preparing their own fish. It was a matter of pride. One of the older boys, who was an Eagle Scout, was able to start a campfire and began preparing one. The other students hung out under the nearest trees and just relaxed.

When the fire was ready, they placed their fish on thin wooden branches that they used as skewers. In no time, the fish was cooked and ready to eat.

Miss Clouder unpacked boxes of graham crackers, bags of marshmallows, and two dozen chocolate bars to make s'mores for dessert. She handed out paper plates. *The woman is amazing!* Maeve admired her teacher's preparedness. She began eating, joining the others around the fire. They were ravenous from the day's activities. When it was time for dessert, ghost stories were on the menu with the s'mores. Some of the oldest students offered to tell their tales first. They were the usual stories that campers shared around a fire.

Maeve whispered to Sylvie, "If we shared our *real* experiences, their hair would stand right up on their heads!"

Sylvie nodded. "I think we should keep them to ourselves. We don't want to scare the heck out of these people, and besides, they would never believe us!"

Maeve agreed, and when it came to their turn to offer a tale, they both declined, claiming they didn't have any stories to offer. They explained their lives were too dull to have any. Miss Clouder accepted that explanation, and in a little while, everyone was off to bed. They were getting up early the next day to go tubing on the river that was about a mile further up the mountain. Maeve took a brief look around the area and listened intently for unwelcome sounds before climbing into her tent and allowing herself to sleep.

Early Sunday morning, the campers were almost finished eating breakfast. Miss Clouder outlined the expectations for the day, and everyone was excited. They packed up the few necessities that they would need for the hike to the river and were eager to begin their walk. They put out the fire and began their trek. After about half an hour, the campers passed a beautiful waterfall on the left. The rushing water was cooling, and the scene was straight out of a Bob Ross painting. They lingered for a few minutes to rest and then continued to the river.

Arriving at the river, they watched as earlier arrivals were loaded into the tubes and received instructions from the guide at the entrance to the ride. Satisfied that everyone was sufficiently aware of the safety regulations and the rules, Miss Clouder allowed each student to climb into a tube. "I'll meet you at the exit, people. Don't wander away," she called. With that, she got into her own tube as well. All went well, except that at the end of the ride, Miss Clouder, who had a substantial backside, could not get out of her tube. She was stuck! She called for help, and it took two guides to pull her out of it. Miss Clouder was embarrassed, but she was a good sport and laughed along with her students, who could not contain their amusement.

The group began the hike back to the campsite. They stopped by the waterfall to have peanut butter sandwiches that Miss Clouder provided with bottled water. A few of the students had never really been out of Wren Falls, so this weekend was a unique and special experience for them. After about an hour of lazing in the sun by the waterfall, they all began the rest of the hike to the campsite. Swimming was on the schedule for the afternoon, and everyone was looking forward to it. A rustic building not far from the campsite provided restrooms for changing. The students took turns going inside to change their clothes.

"I can't wait to hit the lake," Sylvie said excitedly.

"Me, too," Maeve answered.

"This is like Paradise," Sylvie commented.

"Makes me wonder if everything that happened before wasn't real, just my imagination," Maeve added. "But I'm a little worried being out here, so far from town."

"I know what you mean," Sylvie responded. "It's so peaceful here. I'm more relaxed than I've been in months. I can't believe we'll run into that beast out here, especially with so many of us together in a large group."

They headed back to join the group. Soon, everyone was in the lake, swimming, jumping, playing games, and doing a lot of other water-related activities. They stayed in the water for quite a while, with Miss Clouder keeping an eye on them from the shore.

When it was time for dinner, the Eagle Scout built another fire with the wood that the others collected on Saturday. Unbeknownst to the students, Miss Clouder had dragged along a big pot with three boxes of spaghetti and two plastic bottles of tomato sauce in her pack. When she pulled them out, the group gasped! They couldn't believe their teacher had gone to such great lengths for them. A round of applause ensued.

"Hooray for Miss Clouder!" Eagle Scout yelled, and the others joined in.

She blushed and then poured several bottles of water into the pot. After about half an hour, the water began to boil. Fifteen minutes later, the spaghetti was *al dente,* and the teacher heated the sauce with the drained spaghetti. Everyone had seconds. Another dessert of s'mores followed dinner. A second round of ghost stories began. Miss Clouder cut it short, though, saying tomorrow they were leaving after breakfast, and it would be a busy day. They needed their sleep. There were a few protests, but they abruptly stopped when the students heard a loud hissing sound—louder than a single snake would produce. It sounded like there was a large colony of snakes nearby.

"What was that?" one student asked fearfully.

"I'm sure I don't recall any snake activity in this part of the woods," Miss Clouder mentioned, her brow suddenly furrowed. "This is quite unusual. There must be some other explanation. Don't panic, and keep quiet for a minute."

"I hate snakes," one of the girls whispered in a trembling voice.

Maeve and Sylvie looked at each other in consternation. Each could tell what the other was thinking, and it wasn't good. The noise grew louder and seemed to come closer. Suddenly, loud cries came from behind a group of wild oaks. The sound appeared to come from a huge pack of wild dogs howling all at once and it was deafening! It seemed to be getting nearer to the campsite.

"That sounds like wolves," Eagle Scout warned. "I think we'd better leave our things and get out of here, *now!*"

Miss Clouder thought for a moment and then admitted that discretion was the better part of valor. She searched for a flashlight in her bag and turned it on. It didn't light! Miss Clouder checked for a contact problem with the batteries. She shook the flashlight and tried again—no luck. "Yes, people, I do believe it is time for us to go. Leave the fire. It will help light our way, and it will keep predators away from us for the short run. I hope."

The group quickly lined up behind her and hastened down the trail. In a few minutes, the residual light from the fire was gone as it burned itself out, and they stumbled down the hill, tripping and falling. There was some whimpering from the students. The cries of the pack and the hissing of the snakes that seemed to be following them drowned out their sobs. Maeve and Sylvie guessed what was behind them, and they clambered down the mountain in record time. The group just made it to the bus and raced into their seats when an image came into view. Miss Clouder locked the doors in the nick of time as the misshapen beast slammed into the side of the bus, overturning it on the road.

For several minutes, which seemed like hours, the beast clawed at the windows and doors of the bus. It shook the bus violently, trying to get at the prey inside. It howled, growled, and hissed loudly, frightening the bus's occupants. There were moans and shrieks from the students who were still conscious. The others were mercifully quiet. The beast's attack eventually subsided, and it moved off into the bush, lying in wait for the occupants to exit the vehicle, anxious to dismember and digest its prey.

Some time passed before Maeve came to. When she looked around, she observed that only a few students were fully conscious. Miss Clouder slumped over the steering wheel, her eyes closed. Sylvie had a large gash on her forehead but was conscious. A few minutes later, moaning came from the back of the bus, where the boys were sprawled in their seats. Maeve put her index finger up to her lips to show the conscious students they had to be silent if there was any hope of the beast leaving. They had to play dead.

"*Shh*," Maeve addressed the wakening group in a low but firm voice. "Everyone, be quiet! We have to play dead if we want this thing to leave us alone. It isn't interested in dead bodies—only live ones!"

One of the girls in the middle of the bus had been sobbing, but she stopped immediately after registering Maeve's words. The bus became as quiet as a tomb. The students followed Maeve's directions. Stiff and sore, Maeve crawled to the front of the bus and reached Miss Clouder's backpack. She rifled through it, looking for any means of communication she could find. At last, her left hand closed around a cell phone. Maeve recognized what it was but had never used one.

Her father didn't acknowledge the need for the costly phone. The older phones were good enough. Sylvie's father had given her one to use in case of emergencies. *Well, I guess this qualifies as an emergency.* Sylvie had forgotten to pack her phone, but luckily, Miss Clouder had come prepared. *The woman is a marvel, admired* Maeve.

She inched her way back to Sylvie, who was more alert now.

"How does this thing work?" Maeve asked her. Sylvie showed her how to turn on the phone.

"Dial 511 for the Wren Falls Police Department and ask for Sheriff Zen," Maeve whispered. "Tell him we've had a bus crash on Deepwoods Road, and we need two ambulances and backup help. A wild animal attacked our bus, and there are several injured people on board. Tell him *not* to use his sirens or high beams. *Don't* tell him about the beast. Tell him I'll explain everything when he gets here." Maeve had an intuition that the sirens and high beams would attract the beast's attention, and they would be under attack again.

Sylvie nodded in agreement and made the call. Maeve looked around the bus and noticed that in its current position, the Emergency Exit on the ceiling of the bus was now on the side of the bus, making it easier to exit the bus when, or if, the sheriff arrived.

The children on the bus waited silently, some trembling, some sniffling, their eyes betraying their emotions. Miss Clouder began to stir. Maeve crawled over to check on her. When she was sure the teacher was conscious, she told Miss Clouder to rest, stay silent, and wait for help to arrive.

It would be a long night.

Time passed slowly. Maeve worried that the beast, lurking just outside the bus, might ambush the sheriff and his men. She peeked through the bus windows that were now on the ceiling of the vehicle in its current position. She raised her body slowly, stepping on the seats for support, and looked out each window. There was no sign of the creature anywhere.

Relieved, Maeve returned to her seat and waited for the sheriff to arrive. After about another hour, Maeve heard the sound of tires on gravel approaching from behind. Soon, someone began rapping on the side of the bus where the ceiling exit door now lay. When she heard Sheriff Zen's familiar baritone voice on the other side of the door, she exhaled and gingerly opened the door. Maeve was never so happy to see someone as she was Sheriff Zen

"What happened, young lady?" The sheriff looked at the scene in utter disbelief.

"We had an accident."

"That is obvious. Anybody hurt bad?"

"I think Miss Clouder and maybe a few others."

"Well, what in the heck made that huge dent in the side of the bus? Looks like you had a run-in with an elephant," the sheriff continued.

"Something like that," Maeve answered. "I think we'd better get everyone back to town, and we can talk there."

The sheriff and his men loaded Miss Clouder and a few others into ambulances. The rest of the students climbed into police cars for the ride back to Wren Falls. In the distance, they heard the cries of a large pack, which they presumed to be wolves.

By now, Maeve and Sylvie were familiar with the beast's cries. A knowing look passed between them. While some students nodded off on the way home, Maeve busied herself trying to think up an explanation for the sheriff that would be plausible.

"Sylvie, what can we say to the sheriff about what happened? I don't want to tell him about the beast—that would panic the whole town!"

"I think we're going to have to try and convince the others that the creature was really a huge bear."

"That won't be easy," muttered Maeve.

Sylvie rolled over onto her side and began to snore gently next to Maeve, who wondered how she would puzzle out this dilemma.

It was after 11:30 p.m. when the group finally arrived in Wren Falls. The ambulances continued to the nearest hospital. The sheriff brought the rest of the students into his station, where anxious parents awaited their children's arrival. After tearful reunions, the sheriff sent them to their respective homes, saying that statements could be provided the next morning. Only Maeve's father couldn't be reached, so Sylvie's dad took her home, and she spent the night on Sylvie's couch, feeling safe and warm. She was too tired to dream and fell into a deep sleep.

Sylvie's dad dropped Maeve off at her home on his way to work the next day. She entered the house quietly, hoping not to disturb her father while he was sleeping. But she was too late. She could hear cupboard doors banging and loud cursing coming from the kitchen. Maeve walked into the kitchen and said, "Hi, Pa."

"Where the heck have you been?" yelled her father. "Don't you know a man needs a good breakfast to start his day, and you layin' around in bed 'til all hours? Your damned dog has been whining for an hour 'cause he needs to go out, and where are you? You're just a waste of human seed, you are."

Her father hadn't even noticed that she was out all night. He was probably too drunk to be aware of that fact, and even if he was aware she wasn't home, Maeve doubted he would care. He was only interested in his own needs.

"I'll take Pooch out for a quick walk so he can do his business outside, and then I'll be back to make you breakfast, Pa." She got a curt grunt in reply.

Maeve took the leash and her dog outside just in time, as she could taste the salty tears that rolled down her cheeks and onto her lips.

He doesn't care about me. I wish I had a dad like Sylvie's who was there for her all the time. She wiped away her tears and led Pooch back into the house, where she laid out some food and water for him. Then she set about making some oatmeal for herself and her pa.

"About damned time," he grumbled.

"Sorry, Pa." She turned away and ate her meal in silence.

Chapter 11

The next morning, the ambulatory students of Miss Clouder's class, minus Miss Clouder, assembled with their parents in Sheriff Zen's office. The Sheriff asked the group to describe the events of the previous evening.

"There was a huge snake head outside my window!" yelled one girl.

"Loud growling noises were coming from my side of the bus," added one of the boys.

"Before the bus was hit hard and turned over, there was a scratching sound from my side of the bus," said another.

"I can describe it, too," added one of the other girls. "It was a monster! It was big and had a snake's head and a lion's backside! It had the body of a leopard, but it was crazy shaped! The growling was really loud!"

"Wait a minute! Wait a minute!" yelled the sheriff. "You can't all speak at once. And you can't all be right! We have snakes in our woods, but nothing like what you described! I'm sure the dark woods and your imaginations were playing with your minds. We call it mass hysteria, and in these cases, eyewitness accounts vary a great deal. I think the most likely scenario was a huge bear that growled and scratched at the bus."

"No, no!" yelled the girl with the most accurate description of the beast. "You're not listening. I'm right. For sure!"

At this point, Maeve intervened. "We should consider what the sheriff is saying. As a hobby, I've looked up a number of unsolved cases in the Historical Society records, and most of the eyewitness accounts were unreliable because they varied so much. A huge, angry bear is probably the best explanation."

Maeve desperately wanted to convince the others that she was correct. She did not want them going into town and spreading rumors about the beast. It would likely cause panic amongst the residents and wreak havoc in the town. She looked at Sylvie for corroboration, and Sylvie complied.

"Maeve's right. It was too dark to see what rammed us, but the most logical explanation is the bear." The others grumbled, but most seemed to accept her theory and started to leave for home. Only the girl who gave such a vivid description of the beast seemed reluctant.

"Mom, I'm sure I'm right," she insisted.

"I'm sure you *believe* you are, dear, but the sheriff has much more experience in these matters. We need to turn the page." Speaking to the sheriff, she added, "I guarantee my daughter's imagination will not lend any further confusion to this investigation." She turned her daughter in the direction of the door, and they finally exited the police station.

Maeve and Sylvie exhaled sighs of relief.

Sheriff Zen sat back in his office chair and scratched his head. *What could have caused such damage to a solidly built school bus?* Something was nagging at him. Perhaps it was the various descriptions of the creature. The experience definitely shook up the kids. Annabeth Morgan's description was particularly unsettling. Part leopard, part lion? Either the girl was crazy, or her imagination was off like a runaway train. Still, he had a niggling feeling that he should check out the accident scene during the daylight hours, and with that in mind, he called his two best deputies, Henry and Don, into his office.

"Boys," instructed the sheriff, "Just to be sure we've covered the ground completely, so to speak, I want you two to go out to Deepwoods Road and look for any evidence of a creature that could have overturned that darn school bus. We can't close this case proper 'til we find out what really happened that night."

The deputies nodded and exited the police station. They took the department's pickup truck, two rifles, evidence bags, a cell phone, snacks, and bottled water. Next, they headed up to the scene of the incident.

"Don't know what we're gonna find out there. Nothin' out there but woods and critters."

"That's for sure," said the other. "but it's a nice day for a ride, and we ain't got much to do in town." His partner laughed, and the two drove straight to the site of the bus accident.

When the deputies arrived at the scene, they climbed out of the truck and began to search the ground. They overturned anything that looked suspicious and noticed a snake trail that went right through the road. The deputy with the cell phone took a picture of the trail.

"The snake that left that trail must've been a big sucker."

"Glad I missed *that* show." The other nodded his head in agreement.

Pointing at the hoof prints, the first deputy turned to his partner. "Whoa, look at these," he took a step back, whipping out his phone again and snapping away at the unusual prints on the floor of the woods.

"These must belong to a huge stag. I wouldn't want to get in *his* way."

"No, siree," the second deputy concurred. "Butso far, these ain't unusual animals to find in our woods. And I don't see no sign of a bear at all."

"Mebbe that girl, Annabeth, was just playin' us."

"Mebbe so, but I think we gotta' look again, just to be sure."

Several minutes later, the first deputy called out, "Hold it there, Henry! I found a strange mess of bloody hair under that bunch of leaves. Have a look."

Henry looked at a clump of bloody light brown hair that didn't look like any bear hair he'd ever seen. "We need to get this back to town and have the sheriff look at it. Put it in an evidence bag and keep it safe from contamination. Maybe he knows what animal it's from."

"Right," said Don. They wrapped up their exploration of the site, climbed into the pickup, and drove back to town. The two deputies were eager to share what they found with the sheriff.

Sheriff Zen was impressed with their thoroughness and checked the photos first.

"We have plenty of stags and snakes here in the mountains. Nothing unusual here except the size," Sheriff Zen commented. "Those hooves have to belong to some big stag, and the snake impression is huge—looks like a supersized boa or python. We don't have those in the Catskill Mountains, boys. We need to keep an eye out for any sightings that fit these prints. Check with the forestry people. Mebbe they've found prints that look like these."

"Yes, sir," answered Henry and Don in unison.

"Look at this, boss," added Henry. He pulled out the hair sample and showed it to the sheriff.

"Hmm," said the lawman. "This here don't look like it's from any animal living around these parts, boys. I'm gonna' send it to the crime lab in Kingston and see what they come up with. Sure is a puzzling case." He shook his head in bewilderment. He thanked the deputies and sent them to check on Miss Clouder, who was still hospitalized. One boy, who suffered a broken leg, had already returned home.

The sheriff plunked himself back down into his chair. *What could have caused the bus to tip over? Was there some creature roaming the woods that no one had seen yet?* The sheriff was aware of the Bigfoot rumors in the Pacific Northwest, but had always discounted them. *Was some undiscovered creature in the Catskills capable of doing such damage?* He was troubled by the conflicting images of hooves, snake trails, and unidentifiable hair. He sat back in his chair to relax his mind.

A good nap was in order.

The next few days passed uneventfully. The sheriff continued his investigation and waited for lab results. Maeve and Sylvie went back to researching unsolved cases in the Historical Society library. They flipped through the pages of the old news stories until Sylvie called out to her friend.

"Maeve, wasn't your mom's name Alice Newell?"

"Yes, why?"

"There's a story here about her death. I didn't know her killer was never found. I'm so sorry, Maeve."

"I was very young when she died, but I do remember that. Show me that story."

The details of the story were gruesome. They seemed familiar somehow. Reading the story made Maeve relive the event and created a sadness that was overwhelming. As she read the account, Maeve's throat ran dry, and her heart began pounding. She remembered the casket was closed, and she remembered the funeral director's words, *"Not much left of her."* Her father went off the deep end with his drinking. Maeve also had a snippet of a memory of her grandfather regaling guests with his Celtic stories, in a more jovial manner than she would have expected. It seemed nothing was ever right again after her mother's death.

Maeve's head was spinning. Fog enshrouded her brain. She couldn't think straight. Her gut clenched, and her pupils dilated. She had difficulty making her limbs move, and she was nauseous. She had to get out of there. She excused herself, collected her supplies, and stumbled out of the library.

"Maeve, are you okay?" Sylvie called as Maeve ran out the library door.

"Fine," Maeve called to her, but it was clear that her response was not truthful, as she left the Historical Society for home.

"Call you later," she mumbled to Sylvie.

What had happened to Alice Newell? Why didn't my father ever mention Alice after she was buried? She suddenly recalled the details of Elizabeth Newell's passing so many years earlier. *Was Alice's death connected in some way to Elizabeth's? The descriptions of the victims' bodies were very similar. What could have wreaked such havoc on these two women, so many years apart?*

Maeve had a pounding headache. Her father wouldn't be home before the wee hours of the morning, if at all. For some reason, which she could not fathom, Maeve did not really want to see him.

Chapter 12

Sheriff Zen was due to receive the results on the strange hair sample he had given the lab that afternoon. In the meantime, he wanted to interview Annabeth Morgan again. The case of the school bus accident had gone cold, and he was fresh out of leads. The girl seemed very certain of what she had seen, and he reckoned it would be worthwhile to have another talk with her.

The lawman drove up the driveway of her home, noticing the beautiful Spanish tile roof and the pavers on the walkway. Her father was a successful, strait-laced lawyer. And her mother was the president of the Wren Falls Community Improvement Project—quite obsessed with researching ways to beautify the old town by importing a variety of plants and shrubs. She was definitely not a fan of suspending her disbelief in *any* situation. They were a couple very grounded in reality and not the kind of people who would indulge a child in fantasy. The mother struck him as a very no-nonsense sort who was displeased by her daughter's version of the incident. Sheriff Zen rang the bell, and Mr. Morgan escorted him into the study.

"You're here to see Annabeth, aren't you, Sheriff?" Mr. Morgan began. "I hope you can knock some sense into my little girl. Honestly, I don't know where she comes up with her bizarre ideas sometimes." He grimaced.

"I'm just here to get to the bottom of things, Mr. Morgan. I'll listen to her version of the story and make a judgment."

"Hmph...story it is," grumbled Mr. Morgan.

"I don't know where that imagination comes from, certainly not from her mother or me."

"No, I reckon it's her own." The sheriff believed there probably wasn't a scintilla of imagination between the two of them.

"Here she comes now. Good luck with her," Mr. Morgan added, and left the room. A few minutes passed, and Annabeth came into view with Mrs. Morgan. She sat herself down on a heavily upholstered burgundy wing chair, and her mother sat opposite her on a matching loveseat.

"Good afternoon, Annabeth, Mrs. Morgan," began the sheriff. "I've come to clear up a few details from your statement, Annabeth. How are you today?"

"Fine, Mr. Zen."

"*Sheriff* Zen," corrected Mrs. Morgan. "Let's remember our manners, Annabeth,"

Annabeth released a deep sigh and said, "Fine. *Sheriff* Zen," with emphasis on the title.

"Let's move on," interjected the sheriff. "Why don't you tell me what happened the night of the bus accident, Annabeth?"

"I already have at the police station."

Her mother stiffened. Noticing this, Sheriff Zen asked if he could speak to Annabeth privately for a few minutes. Mrs. Morgan looked uncomfortable with the suggestion and began, "I don't think that's advisable, Sheriff. I would prefer to be here."

Sheriff Zen nodded sympathetically. "I totally understand a mother's need to be supportive of her child, but I assure you, I will be gentle in my questioning, and your presence could be distracting for Annabeth. After all, we just want to get to the truth, don't we?"

"I guess so." Mrs. Morgan rose with great reluctance from her loveseat and slowly made her way to the door, looking back frequently at her daughter.

Sheriff Zen turned back to Annabeth. "Now, why don't you describe the events of that night for me, Annabeth?"

"Okay." Warming to the topic, she popped a piece of blue bubble gum into her mouth and began cracking it as she spoke.

Sometime later, the sheriff had Annabeth's detailed version of the accident, complete with an oddly shaped monster that had the backside of a lion, the body of a leopard, hooves, and the head of a giant snake—a monster who rammed the side of the bus with such force that it overturned the vehicle and caused several injuries. Generously, she also credited Maeve with getting help for the group and bravely checking for the monster's presence by looking through the bus windows.

"So, Maeve Newell also observed this monster?" asked Sheriff Zen.

"I don't know. It was gone when Maeve looked out of the windows, but she was sure brave."

"And you are absolutely sure that this creature looked as you described, Annabeth?"

Annabeth crossed her arms over her chest. "I am *absolutely* sure, Sheriff," and she cracked her gum one more time before spitting it into her open palm and placing it carefully underneath the top of the antique marble table beside her chair.

The sheriff thanked Annabeth, exited the study, tipped his hat to her anxious-looking mother, and quickly left the building. "Man," he said to no one in particular. "That kid is some piece of work."

He climbed into his truck, went home for lunch, and figured that he had earned an afternoon nap, which he took advantage of as soon as the last crumbs of his tuna on rye sandwich disappeared.

Chapter 13

Maeve had been looking forward to her visit with "Aunt" Nelda for weeks. Nelda had invited Maeve to spend the night after learning of the bus accident. Maeve was thrilled at the prospect of spending time with her "Aunt", particularly as her relationship with her dad had deteriorated lately. She needed some distance from him and Nelda's place was the perfect spot to enjoy some relaxation and good conversation. She looked forward to being with someone who showed her affection and cared about her. It was a great escape from her run-down cottage and Pa.

Maeve had a lot of questions for her "Aunt" and always enjoyed Nelda's company. Aunt Nelda's home was a Victorian, filled with fascinating antiques and knick-knacks scattered throughout. There were oil paintings of ancestors, Persian rugs, perfume bottles in different sizes and shapes, and a collection of other intriguing items that Maeve never got tired of studying.

Aunt Nelda also had fabulous costumes and exotic clothing that she let Maeve try on and pretend to walk the runway like a fashion model. Maeve never got bored listening to stories about her travels and the famous, and infamous, characters she met along the way. It seemed to Maeve that Aunt Nelda had lived a dozen lifetimes in the span of one.

To top it all off, Aunt Nelda was an amazing chef. She could and did prepare gourmet meals ranging from Chinese delicacies to Middle Eastern cuisine, with stops in Europe, South America, and Africa, along the way. It was an adventure spending time with her in her abode, which didn't happen often enough for Maeve.

On this particular evening, Maeve arrived early at Nelda's. She was so anxious to get there, she didn't pay attention to the time. Aunt Nelda was also great about letting Pooch stay with Maeve. He didn't bother Nelda. She enjoyed his company. So, Maeve and Pooch let themselves in and walked into her living room.

There, before a floor-to-ceiling gilt-edged antique mirror, was Aunt Nelda in an exotic Arabian costume speaking in a language Maeve couldn't identify. She had her eyes closed, her arms outstretched, and she seemed to be reciting an incantation.

"Aunt Nelda," called Maeve. "What are you doing?"

Visibly shaken, Aunt Nelda jolted out of her trance. "My word, girl, you startled me. I was meditating and doing my personal chanting. What time is it? Aren't you early?"

Embarrassed, Maeve apologized for having caught Nelda off guard. "Sorry, Aunt Nelda. I was so excited to spend time with you, I forgot to check the time."

"No matter, child. I'm delighted to have the chance to visit with you. Let me change out of these clothes."

"You can stay in them, if you want," said Maeve. "I love looking at all the bright colors and how the material moves with you."

"That's silk, my dear—one of my favorite fabrics," Nelda answered. "Very well, I shall remain in them just for you."

"What are we eating tonight?" Maeve's stomach grumbled. "I brought food for Pooch, so I'll just set it down in the kitchen for him."

"Perfect," said Nelda. We are having moussaka from Greece tonight with a glorious salad with feta cheese, spanakopita, and baklava."

"Yum," said Maeve. That sounds wonderful!"

"Come sit in the dining room, Maeve. We have so much to catch up on. Tell me everything that's been happening in your life since we last met,"

Nelda prompted. "I'll just start serving the food, and we can talk while we eat."

Maeve didn't know where to begin.

"How is your father, Maeve?" Nelda asked.

"He's getting worse. He's almost never home, he's always drunk, and he doesn't even know I exist. Since Mom died, it's like I don't have a father. I'm practically invisible to him. I might as well be living by myself."

"I miss your mom, too, honey. We were like sisters. She would not want her little girl living such a lonely existence. You must come to me when you need something, even if it's just to talk. We will meet more often, and I think it's about time that I have a talk with your father. I have been too distracted by other things, and I'm sorry." She looked down at the clasped fingers in her lap and sighed.

"It's okay, Aunt Nelda. You are very busy. I'll be all right. By the way, I have a new friend at school."

"Tell me all about your new friend, and let's dig in!" Aunt Nelda remarked as she served the first course. Maeve then launched into a description of Sylvie and her father, relating some of the details of their relationship in between bites of salad. They spent the rest of the evening in deep conversation until fatigue overtook her body.

She excused herself and let sleep overtake her in the big four-poster bed she loved.

The interlude at Aunt Nelda's was a brief respite from the dreariness of life in the Newell household. Maeve's daily existence began with chores and making meals for her dad and herself. She fed Pooch, gave him fresh water, and took him on a brief walk. Then she was able to spend the rest of the day on the things that interested her most. She was about to call Sylvie to ask her for plans when there was a sharp rap on the door. *Who could that be?*

Maeve cursed the fact that her father still hadn't put a peephole in the door. She never could identify who was standing there and would have liked to have had an eye on whoever was out there, especially now, with the beast on the loose.

"Maeve, are you home?" She recognized Sheriff Zen's deep voice and opened the front door. "Oh, hello, Maeve. If you don't mind, I'd like a word with you about what happened in the woods a few nights ago."

Damn, Maeve thought to herself, *when will this end? I really don't want to talk to him about what happened.*

"Um... Didn't Sylvie already answer all your questions, Sheriff?"

"I did talk to her, Maeve, but I really want to hear your version of what took place."

"Sure, Sheriff," Maeve answered reluctantly. "Come on in. Would you care for a drink? Coffee? Water?"

"No thanks, Maeve. Just some information will do."

Maeve showed Sheriff Zen into the living room and offered him the best of the ragged chairs to sit on. He made himself comfortable.

"Tell me, Maeve, to the best of your recollection, what happened in the woods when you and your friends were getting ready to board the school bus the other night?"

Maeve cleared her throat. She could detect a lump forming in her stomach. For a fleeting moment, she considered telling him the truth. She quickly discounted that idea, fearing that others in the town would mock her, saying she was nuts, just like her crazy father. That was something she could not bear, so she stuck to the story that Sylvie and she had concocted.

"We were walking down the mountain to board the school bus when we heard some loud noises, what sounded like a pack of wolves howling in the night. We hurried down to the bus and rushed inside. Miss Clouder just had time to slam the doors shut when a large animal crashed into the bus. I'm pretty sure it was a bear clawing the side of the bus and eventually, ramming it so hard that it turned the bus over on its side. After a while, it went away. I climbed up on one of the seats to look out the bus's windows to be sure if it was really gone. It was. I used Miss Clouder's cell phone to call you for help, and that's about all I can remember," she finished.

"Did you actually get a good look at the animal, Maeve?" the sheriff asked.

"No, sir," she answered.

"So, what makes you so sure it was a bear?"

"It seems like the only explanation that makes sense." Maeve fidgeted with her fingers on the hem of her shirt.

"Annabeth Morgan is still convinced that it was some kind of unusual beast that looked to be part lion, part leopard, part snake, and part deer."

"Sheriff, how crazy does that sound to you? I think she was just shaken up and her imagination got carried away." Maeve had difficulty looking the sheriff in the eye.

"I understand that is a possibility. Is there anything you'd like to add to your statement?"

"I think that's everything, Sheriff. I hope Miss Clouder is released soon from the hospital, and I'm glad the other kids are all home now. Do you know how she's doing?" Maeve tried to change the subject.

"I believe she's coming home tomorrow, Maeve. I'll tell her you asked about her," he added.

Sheriff Zen rose to take his leave, and Maeve showed him to the door. *That little girl is sure nervous. Poor thing, living with that drunken father of hers and no mother must be tough. Seeing me at the door couldn't have helped.* His eyes lingered on the worn furniture and then onto Maeve's unusual pallor. "Are you okay, Maeve? Is there anything else you want to tell me?"

"No, Sheriff. That's everything." Maeve closed the door and bolted it after the sheriff stepped outside. She sighed with relief and hoped he bought her explanation. Sheriff Zen climbed into his police car and reasoned that Maeve was probably right about Annabeth. A bear was the most likely explanation.

Chapter 14

Alice Newell had just returned from her picnic with Collum Carmichael. Things had gotten out of hand, and Alice regretted her interlude with him under the old oak tree. After all, she loved her husband. She was feeling neglected and was thrilled to have some male attention. She would have to tell Collum that the romance was over.

Will watched as Alice went out to her garden and began weeding. His hatred of her burned like a hot coal in his stomach. His thoughts went to his son and how he was being cuckolded.

"Nobody makes a fool of my son," he growled out loud.

He was sure of what he had to do to make Alice pay for her indiscretions. He'd done it once before with Elizabeth. It would be easier the second time. Will planned his revenge for the next day and set about putting things in order.

The following afternoon, Alice told Will that she was going to help Collum plant a new species of evergreen in his garden. She would be back in a few hours. Alice had planned to tell Collum that their relationship must remain platonic now and forever. She accepted that he would not be happy about it, but it was the right thing to do if she wanted her marriage to have a chance of success.

Rocking on Alice's porch, Will waited for her to return. He passed the time reading the local papers as twilight settled in. James would be attending a meeting at the local tavern. Afterwards, he and his pa were to meet up at the bonfire. Alice had no interest in attending the Samhain ceremonies. When she retired to her bedroom, Will returned to his own home, went downstairs to the basement, and began his preparations for her punishment.

First, he donned his black robes and lit candles around the room. When he was satisfied that the ambience was perfect, he began his incantation:

Nomine Demonicus voyis ayudan
Revanicle mewyzicor dormiculus
Questoribin Anigamicus

After the sixth time reciting the incantation, Will removed his robes, blew out the candles, and made his way to the bonfire celebration of Samhain. An hour after his arrival, his son joined him in the crowd, oblivious to what was taking place in his home. Ten-year-old Maeve was spending the night at Aunt Nelda's, who regaled her with stories of past Samhain celebrations she had enjoyed.

The beast savagely tore the limbs from Alice. Her screams and pleas went unnoticed since all her neighbors were at the bonfire. She bled out quickly as the creature tossed her severed arms and legs about the room. The monster devoured most of Alice. In its fury, blood splattered on the walls, the floor, and the furniture. It dragged her remains to a nearby creek, where her horror-stricken face floated on the surface. When James returned home after the bonfire, he saw the trail of blood leading out of the house and raced inside, frantically searching for his wife.

The results of his search sent him into shock. He staggered out of the house, barely breathing, his eyes glazed over. A neighbor met him at the door and told James of his own gruesome discovery after following the massive blood trail leading from James's home to the creek. He was almost incoherent and badly shaken. The neighbor's wife called the police, who in turn brought Alice's remains to the town's funeral director. Upon hearing the news, all the air escaped from James's lungs. His heart skipped several beats, and he collapsed in the nearest chair, but not before taking a giant swig of his homemade whiskey.

The gravediggers buried Alice under her favorite old oak tree, and townspeople came to pay their respects at the house. Will was busy regaling the visitors with stories of old Celtic myths and legends, not speaking much about Alice at all. Maeve caught a bit of his stories, but mostly she clung to Pooch for comfort. Her father was half drunk, moaning about the loss of his saintly wife. After the funeral, the empty house lost all its warmth.

Sheriff Zen and his deputies investigated Alice's death but found no clues leading to a viable suspect or conviction. Rumors circulated in town, but no one dared repeat them in public. The fact that the horrific event occurred during Samhain caused some to think her death was related to ancient myths, but speaking these theories aloud was believed to bring forth the evil beings of the Celtic legends. The sheriff, a rational man, dismissed this speculation and concluded that Alice's demise was the result of a random animal attack. The unsolved cold case, number 666, was closed. It remained so for the next five years, until Maeve and Sylvie began to delve deeper into the bizarre crimes uncovered in the records of the Wren Falls Historical Society.

Sheriff Zen eagerly opened the envelope from the testing lab with the crystal letter opener that his wife gave him last Christmas. He was really curious to learn just what kind of animal the hair sample came from. The deputies had started a pool to pick the correct animal, and they had both bet on wolves. The sheriff's money was on a large bear.

"No wolf I've ever seen could have the strength to overturn a school bus."

To which they argued that it might have been a pack of wolves, which probably could have accomplished the feat. The sheriff was so sure he would win this bet that he had already made dinner reservations to take his wife to her favorite Wren Falls restaurant there were only two choices, for her birthday.

He opened the letter from the lab and scanned it quickly. When he came to the critical paragraph, he gasped. "What in tarnation is this about?" he yelled. The deputies came running and asked what was wrong. Sputtering, the chief handed Don the letter. Henry read it over his shoulder.

It said, "The DNA results prove to a ninety-nine percent degree of accuracy that the strand of hair submitted by Sheriff Zen of the Wren Falls Police Department belongs to a lion."

The three lawmen looked at each other in shock, their mouths hanging open. When the sheriff came to his senses, he picked up the phone and cancelled his dinner reservation.

After the initial shock, Sheriff Zen decided a second interview with Maeve Newell was in order. The girl had poo-pooed Annabeth's description of the creature, but it seemed like Annabeth was definitely on the right track. *Was Maeve lying to him? Was she just mistaken? Did she see the creature or not?* The sheriff was going to get to the bottom of this mystery if it was the last thing he did. On top of that, his wife was already holding him to his birthday dinner proposal, and he would have to shell out the money for it himself. The sheriff was not in a good mood when he drove up to Maeve's home.

Chapter 15

*R*ap! *Rap*! *Rap*! The sheriff knocked impatiently on Maeve's door. There was no response. She obviously wasn't home, and he would have to come back. His mood darkened as he climbed back into his squad car. As he pulled away, Maeve came out from behind her living room club chair and breathed a sigh of relief. She was in no frame of mind to be re-interrogated, and when she saw the police car pull onto her property, she guessed that the sheriff had gotten his lab results and was coming to confront her. He expected them any day, and from the look of his facial expression, the results arrived today, and he was none too pleased.

What could she tell the sheriff? In the end, she decided to stick to her story. She didn't want to feed into the town gossip and cause a real panic. Even more, she didn't want to be mocked by the townspeople as a crazy girl from a crazy family. She was aware of what everyone thought of her father. Also, she didn't want the sheriff to think she was a liar. She was better off telling him what she believed he spotted and letting him conclude that she was mistaken. Assuming she had resolved a thorny problem, she decided to take Pooch for a walk. It was getting closer to dusk, so she was mindful that it would have to be a short walk. She got his leash and opened the door to the cottage. She was stunned to find herself looking straight into the face of...the sheriff!

"Hello, Maeve. I'm back to check if, maybe, you were available now. You might have been doing laundry or watching TV and didn't hear me rapping on your door before. I guess this would be a good time for us to review your statement." Moving nonchalantly, he stepped inside her home. In fact, the sheriff had suspected that Maeve might be avoiding him, so he drove around the block, waited ten minutes, and then returned to her house. He waited on her front steps quietly for a short while, figuring that she might be coming outside for a dog walk at this time of the day, and he was right.

Maeve's face turned a particular shade of bright pink. "Of course, Sheriff. Have a seat in the living room."

Sheriff Zen made himself comfortable.

"As you are aware, Maeve, I've been waiting for the analysis of a hair sample found at the scene of the bus accident. The results came back yesterday from the lab in Kingston and said that the hair was from a lion. It appears Annabeth was right in at least one respect. What do you have to say about that?"

"I don't know, Sheriff. I didn't actually see the animal, but the bear explanation makes the most sense to me."

"Do you have any other information you would like to share, Maeve?" the sheriff asked.

"No, sir. As I said, I didn't get a good look at the animal, but it had to be big and strong. I don't think a lion would be big enough to overturn a bus, and besides, we have no lions in this area."

"Very well, Maeve. Since you have nothing new to add, I'll be off. Take care of yourself and give my regards to your dad."

"I will, sir. Thank you."

The sheriff got up to leave and Maeve exhaled. She didn't know where to go with this new information. She had to talk to Sylvie.

As the sheriff opened his car door, a loud noise that sounded like the cries of a large pack of dogs seemed to be drawing nearer. He shivered and closed the door quickly after he got into the driver's seat. *What the heck could that be? What in tarnation was going on in the sleepy town of Wren Falls?*

He didn't know but damned if he wasn't going to find out.

Maeve called Sylvie on the phone, and they arranged to meet at the Historical Society the next afternoon. There was a lot that Maeve wanted to discuss with her, and they hadn't had much time together lately. During the summer months, Sylvie's dad liked to take his daughter on short weekend trips to go hiking in the mountains, tubing, or fishing in the next county. Maeve really missed Sylvie on these occasions. She had become used to having a friend around, and returning to an isolated existence on the weekends was depressing. *My dad wouldn't think of spending time alone with me. He's too busy with his still.* "Thank God for you, boy," she said to Pooch as she bent down to pet him. Pooch licked her face as if he completely understood her words.

The next afternoon, the girls greeted each other with a warm hug. Apart from their time in school together, they hadn't had much opportunity to hang out. Together, they fit like a complete puzzle. Apart, there was always a piece missing. Sylvie surprised Maeve with one of her father's Betty Crocker brownies, which Maeve wolfed down in less than a minute. "Yum," she mumbled, crumbs dripping from her mouth. "Please thank your dad, Sylvie. That was delicious!"

Sylvie grinned with pleasure. "I will. He'll be thrilled you liked it."

The two teenagers climbed the stairs to the Historical Society and entered its library. As before, it was sparsely populated, enabling the girls to chat quietly without disturbing others. On their way into the library, Maeve filled Sylvie in on the sheriff's visit and his news about the hair sample and the lab's analysis. "Great said Sylvie. "Just what we needed. He'll probably be at my house next. He's got his teeth sunk into this case so deep, he's not going to let go of it easily."

"Yes." Maeve turned to her friend. "You can just tell him what I told him. You didn't get a good look at the animal, and a giant bear makes the most sense to you. What can he say to that?"

"I just don't like the fact that he won't drop it," Sylvie responded. "We obviously haven't seen the last of him. Damn that Annabeth Morgan!" she shouted.

Sylvie eventually calmed down. "I just can't help wondering about your mom's unsolved death and Elizabeth Newell's unsolved death. I think there's some connection between them."

"You're probably right, Sylvie," Maeve admitted. "I've been thinking a lot about that, too. Maybe we should look into both and search for similarities."

"Yeah, we might actually find some clues as to how and why these deaths happened," added Sylvie. "Are you up to investigating your mom's death? It must be a painful subject for you."

"It is. But at least if I can help solve the mystery of what happened to her, I'll be grateful that I was able to do something for her, you know? When she died, I was too young to do anything except cry."

Sylvie watched Maeve's face carefully during this discussion. "I get it, Maeve. So, let's go back to the files on the computer and compare the two cases. Maybe we can find some connections or similarities between these two women's deaths."

Maeve agreed, and the two girls set about combing through the news stories to unearth any facts that might help. At the end of the afternoon, they came up with the following conclusions:

Both women were "Newells."

Both women were attacked when they were alone in their homes.

Both women were attacked on October 31st, during the Samhain celebrations.

Both bodies were found in the same condition.

Both women were believed to have been attacked by a vicious animal.

Both cases were unsolved and considered "cold cases."

Sylvie and Maeve had been so focused on their research that they didn't notice the hours slipping by. Finally, Maeve looked up and noticed that the library's clock registered 4:30 p.m. "Oh, my gosh! Sylvie, look at the time!"

Sylvie looked at the clock, gasped, and then the two girls looked at each other.

They both realized the danger in walking outside the town limits. Fortunately, it was still summer, and the days were longer.

"It'll be light for a while, but still, we'd better get going," warned Maeve.

"For sure," Sylvie agreed, and they gathered up their books and papers, heading for the exit door.

After walking for a while, they came to the fork in the road where they parted for their respective homes. Today, they quickened their steps, anxious to get to their destinations before anything bad could happen. They said their "goodbyes" and sprinted towards their safety zones.

Chapter 16

When the beast emerged from its hiding place, Maeve saw it out of the corner of her eye. She was closest to the cut-off to Aunt Nelda's house, so she ran in that direction, hoping to reach shelter before the beast caught up with her. Hooves pounded on the path behind her. The cries and growls increased in volume as the creature approached. Finally, the hissing of the snake over her left shoulder seemed closer. She was aware that if she turned to look, she would freeze in fear and all would be lost. Sweat poured down her face, interfering with her vision. Her heart beat erratically and rapidly, while her mouth ran dry. She hoped her legs wouldn't give out. She was almost at Aunt Nelda's. She could glimpse the home, defended by a stone wall, about half a mile further down the road. If she could just make it...she prayed fervently for the help of a higher power.

By some miracle, Maeve barged through the front door and slammed it shut just before the beast reached her. Maeve appreciated the fact that Aunt Nelda never locked her door. She shoved the heavy bolt in place and tried to catch her breath as the beast growled and slammed its body against the door in a rage. Maeve's limbs shook uncontrollably. She saw black spots in front of her eyes. Maeve couldn't catch her breath and began to experience her consciousness slipping away. Maeve stayed away from the windows and hid behind a marble column in the living room. She was shivering, and her hands were shaking. After what seemed like an hour but was really only about ten minutes, the beast slithered away, looking for other prey. Only then could Maeve exhale.

When she got her land legs back, and noticed her energy returning, Maeve ran upstairs to Nelda's sitting room and observed Nelda from the back, in one of her trances. Maeve watched her shimmying, fluid movements, and her expressive hands in the air. She seemed unaware of Maeve's presence. Loud reggae music blasted from Nelda's MP3 player, Nelda was not able to acknowledge Maeve calling her until Maeve raised her voice—a lot! "Aunt Nelda!" she shouted, and that broke through the trance, causing Nelda to turn around.

It was then that Maeve got her second shock of the day. The woman who faced her looked nothing like Aunt Nelda. She was old, with wrinkled skin and white hair covered by a shawl. She lacked the fine facial features of Nelda. Stray hairs escaped from her chin.

"Who-o-o are you?" asked Maeve in a shaky voice.

"I am Goody Webster, child. I'm well aware of who *you* are," answered the old woman in a scratchy voice.

"I'm looking for my Aunt Nelda," said Maeve.

"Dearest Maeve, you've found her." The old woman cackled uncontrollably.

"What do you mean?" Maeve demanded, stomping her foot. "I want to speak to Aunt Nelda. Where is she? I want Aunt Nelda!"

"Calm down, girl," answered Goody. "I've no use for these histrionics." She shoved her hands into her pockets and pulled out fistfuls of red dust, which she threw into the air. The dust formed spirals around Goody, and in less than a minute, she turned into Nelda.

Maeve just stood there, her mouth agape, staring at her beloved Aunt Nelda. "What is going on? Who is Goody, and why was she here?"

Nelda motioned to a striped Queen Anne chair and said, "Sit, Maeve. I have so much to tell you. You will need to suspend your disbelief because a good deal of what I am going to say will seem unbelievable. I need a bracing cup of strawberry rhubarb tea before we begin. Would you like some?"

"Okay," replied Maeve in a quieter voice than earlier. She had no idea what to expect from Nelda, but it seemed a bracing cup of tea might be what she'd need to calm her jittery nerves. Aunt Nelda left the room for a few minutes and returned with an ornate French teapot and matching cups and saucers on a Louis XIV tray. The tea leaves were already in the cups, so she added the hot water and a bit of sugar.

"Lemon?" she asked Maeve, who shook her head.

"Who is Goody?" Maeve asked again.

"I will tell you a story, Maeve, and you will understand better what you have seen. You may not interrupt me until I am finished, so just listen closely."

"Once, a very long time ago, in the 1600s, there lived a Light Witch who used her magic for good. She created charms and potions for the people of her village who needed help. Perhaps they wanted a child desperately and couldn't have one. Or their crops would not grow, and they were starving. If they came to the Light Witch, she would help them with her magic, and the people were grateful. That is, they were grateful until the Fever came."

"What was the Fever, Aunt Nelda?"

"No interruptions, please. The Fever was an anti-magic, anti-witch feeling that swept over the village and caused the leaders of the village to round up and destroy anyone with magical powers. The people turned against the Light Witch and sentenced her to death. She was hanged by the village leaders and went into the Netherworld. This Light Witch was Goody Webster."

Shock registered on Maeve's face.

"Before she was killed, she entrusted a very important possession to a good man she had become close to in the village. It was a book that had to be kept safe and away from prying eyes. This man was the only human she trusted to watch over the book, and he did so for hundreds of years, keeping the contents away from others who might use it for malicious intent.

"The book contained the secrets of all the evils in the world. Unfortunately, the good man completely transformed when he learned something that enraged him and turned his personality inside out. He was obsessed with revenge. As a result, he used his knowledge from the book for Evil."

"Who was the man, Aunt Nelda?"

"All in good time, Maeve. More tea?"

"No, thank you."

"Through the years," Nelda went on, "Goody appeared to this man and beseeched him not to do evil deeds, but the man was driven to exact vengeance on those he thought betrayed him or his family. Once, she gave in to his pleas for help, and for that she paid a stiff price in the Netherworld. She was forbidden to have any contact with humans for a century."

"She must have been very lonely."

"Yes, she was, since all her earthly life she had lived among people and devoted herself to helping them. Fifty years ago, she was pardoned by the gods and was permitted to live amongst the humans again, provided she remained helpful to them and stayed away from Dark Magic."

"May I ask a question, Aunt Nelda?"

"Yes, child. Now you may ask me anything."

"Who was dancing when I entered the house? Why was Goody in your sitting room? How is she connected to you?" Maeve's mind bubbled over with questions.

Nelda turned to Maeve and gave her a big smile. "You saw me, Maeve. Goody is me."

Maeve stared a moment at Aunt Nelda in shock, before she slid to the floor in a dead faint.

She regained consciousness after Nelda sprinkled cold water on her face, put a stuffed purple pillow under her head, and an ice pack on her forehead.

"What happened?"

"You fainted, my dear. I guess my story had quite an impact on you," Aunt Nelda explained with a concerned look on her face. She lifted Maeve up and settled her in the striped chair. "I'll get you some ice water. That should do the trick."

A few minutes later, Maeve felt stronger and peppered Aunt Nelda with more questions. "Who was the man Goody trusted? What did he do that was evil? What was the book called?".

"That's enough for today, Maeve. We'll continue another time. Not a word to anyone about what I told you. This needs to be kept a secret. There's plenty more to discuss in a future visit, dear," and that was the end of the discussion. Maeve understood Aunt Nelda well enough that when she said "Enough," that would be the end for now.

Maeve wanted to tell Aunt Nelda about the beast, but she was exhausted and wanted to get home before it got late. So, she gave Aunt Nelda a hug, checked the surroundings after she opened the door, and cautiously made her way home to Pooch. When she arrived, Pa was out, and Pooch was sleeping under the kitchen table. Maeve took advantage of the opportunity to get some sleep herself and flopped down on her bed after locking the front door.

Chapter 17

Maeve and Sylvie met to continue their research at the Historical Society the next day. Now that the two cold cases appeared to be connected to Maeve's family history, the research took on greater urgency. They planned to work there for about two hours, grab something quick to eat at Little Piggy's Burger Barn, and then spend the afternoon painting at Sylvie's house. Sylvie had promised to show Maeve how to make a wash with her watercolor paints. Maeve was uncomfortable having Sylvie visit her at her own cottage, fearing that her father would be around in a slovenly state, which would be mortifying.

"Did you get home okay yesterday?" asked Sylvie.

"Not exactly."

"Uh oh, what happened?" Sylvie pressed, fearing the worst.

"When I got to the cut-off to Aunt Nelda's that damned beast jumped out from behind a huge tree trunk on the side of the road and began chasing me."

"Oh, my God!" shrieked Sylvie, which prompted a loud *Shhh!* from the Society librarian. "What did you do?"

"What do you think? I ran like the devil was chasing me. Actually, it *was*!" revealed Maeve. "I ran for Aunt Nelda's house, since it was the closest place I could think of, and I barely made it through her door before that monster crashed right into it!"

Sylvie gasped. "What did you do next?"

"I bolted the door and collapsed into a chair to catch my breath. Then I ran upstairs to find Aunt Nelda. I was terrified!" Maeve shuddered at the recent memory of her narrow escape.

"Oh, my gosh! Oh, my gosh! I should never have left you alone on the road," Sylvie sobbed.

"Don't be ridiculous, Sylvie. How would it have been better if both of us were in that situation? I barely made it to Aunt Nelda's before that creature slammed into her door. It's all right. I'm fine. Calm down and let's get back to work."

"Are you sure you're okay?" Sylvie sniffled. "I would have had nightmares for weeks after that. How'd you sleep?"

"Like a babe, Sylvie," Maeve answered. "When I finally got home, I was too exhausted to dream."

They worked for a while, following up on stories in the news, crosschecking information, and reviewing statements from sources. At one point, Sylvie asked, "So what did you do at your Aunt Nelda's? She's such an interesting person."

Remembering her promise not to reveal anything of their visit to anyone, Maeve said, "Oh, we drank some herbal tea and had a snack. Nelda talked to me about the artifacts in her living room. When I felt better, I looked out of her picture window to check if all was clear. I didn't notice any sign of the beast, so I took a different route home and went to bed after I took Pooch out for a few minutes. No problem."

"You are much braver than I am," Sylvie admitted. "I would have had a meltdown when I got home."

"Not so brave," Maeve confessed. "I had a meltdown at Aunt Nelda's before I saw her."

They both laughed, earning another stern "*Shhhh!*" from the librarian.

They apologized and went back to their research. After a couple of hours, they collected their notebooks, newspaper photocopies, and anything else they had brought with them and walked over to Little Piggy's.

Maeve mused, *It is great having a friend to do things with, finally. This year with Sylvie has changed my life.*

Both girls had worked up a real appetite. "My treat!" yelled Sylvie.

"Thanks!" Maeve grinned. "In that case, I'll have two Little Piggy burgers with lettuce, tomato, pickles, and mayo, one large fries, and a large cola."

Sylvie laughed. "I'll have the same, but cheeseburgers, please," and they both plopped down in a nearby booth and shoved all their work to one side of their booth as they gorged themselves on their lunches. When they were sated, they made their way to Sylvie's home, painted for a while, and ended the day with a competitive game of Monopoly. It was a relaxing afternoon, the kind that kids were supposed to have, instead of the terror-inducing events that stalked them.

At the end of the most relaxing day Maeve had experienced in months, she luxuriated in her favorite worn rocker that her pa had pilfered from Grandpa Will's dilapidated house. It was her father's one generous gesture after Papa Will passed on. James Newell appreciated that Maeve and her grandpa were very close, so he gave her this chair to remember Papa Will. It was a comfort to Maeve when Papa Will's spirit embraced her as she sat alone in her room. Sometimes she would even speak to him when she needed advice. Today was one of those days.

"Grandpa, I'm not sure what to do. Sylvie is my best friend, and I don't want to keep secrets from her. Aunt Nelda made me swear not to tell anyone what she told me, but it doesn't seem right to keep secrets from Sylvie. Sylvie would be honest with me in a situation like this, and I hate the fact that I'm lying to her. She would never tell anyone Aunt Nelda's secret."

As usual, she got no reply.

When she went to sleep that night, Grandpa Will appeared in her dream. His face was distorted and skeletal. Blood was dripping from his swollen lips. He was scowling at Maeve and moving towards her. His black cloak contrasted sharply with the pallor of his skin. Hollow eye sockets completed the horrific image of her desiccated Papa Will. These ghastly images were usually accompanied by bone-chilling cackling that bore no resemblance to Papa Will's voice—the one that Maeve knew and loved.

It was a disturbing dream, and she woke up screaming. There was no one home to calm her or ease her shaking. Only Pooch reacted to her cries, and he climbed up on the bed. He began licking her face while whimpering. Pooch's behavior brought Maeve back to reality. She understood the fright was only in her mind, but, nevertheless, she sobbed into her pillow and prayed for the morning to come.

Maeve was unable to block these dreams from her mind, not even in the daytime. They were getting more and more horrifying. The dreams seemed to center around Papa Will. He appeared more threatening with each dream. His physical appearance continued to deteriorate, and he looked more like death with each occurrence. Maeve couldn't understand why the dreams were becoming increasingly terrifying or why her grandfather was angry with her. They were always so close. Her father never appeared in the dreams. There was no suggestion of his coming to her aid. *Just like in my real life.* Maeve sighed and began to drag herself out of bed to prepare for the day ahead.

Maeve had no idea when the dreams would end. She hoped it would be soon. Every morning, she woke even more exhausted than the night before. It was becoming difficult to focus on school. This situation couldn't go on much longer. She needed a good night's sleep and the energy that came with it.

Chapter 18

Sheriff Zen worried that his investigation into the bus incident was at a standstill. The townspeople were anxious for a final explanation of what happened at the campgrounds. With this new information from the lab, he had to act fast. He couldn't just sit back while a wild lion roamed the forest around Wren Falls. *For God's sake, families camped out there all the time, so did the scout troops and school groups. He couldn't just leave them to the mercy of a hungry lion! And what was up with Maeve? Something about her story just didn't ring true. He would get to the bottom of it, if it was the last thing he did on this Earth!*

The sheriff bolted upright in his chair and decided on action rather than rumination. He called his two best deputies into his office. "Don, Henry! Get your butts in here, pronto!" He decided to be proactive, which improved his mood. His control of the situation was building

"Coming, sir," they answered simultaneously. A moment later, they surrounded his desk like a pair of matching bookends.

"Boys," the Chief commanded, "I want to end the speculation, rumors, and fears in this here community. I want that bus incident explained, and any animal involved in it captured. I don't want another week to pass without some resolution for the townspeople, or they'll be asking for my badge." And he said with a sly look at Don and Henry, "If I go, then you two will be goin' with me."

"Yes, sir!" The duo answered in tandem.

Earlier, the sheriff had shared the lab results with his deputies. "Now, take your weapons and some extra ammo just in case you have to defend yourselves and stake out the area surrounding Deepwoods Road near the campgrounds. I want you to cover a four mile radius from where that bus was found and hide yourselves in the foliage—that means 'camo', boys. Blend in with the trees and the grasses. Don't come back here until that thing is either dead or captured. Either way, bring its body back to town. I need proof that the case is closed. I *need* results and I needed them *yesterday*! Got it?" By now, the sheriff's tone of voice was unmistakable. He was pissed and the deputies knew it.

"Got it, sir," they said.

They left the office immediately to get their gear together and some necessary nutritional supplies like beef jerky, water, chocolate, and cookies. Each simultaneously removed a moderately clean handkerchief from a pants pocket and wiped the sweat off his brow.

"I never seen him so wound up," Don griped to his partner.

"Me, neither. We better not show our faces 'til this creature, whatever it is, is history," agreed Henry. "D'ya think he was serious about us losin' our jobs?"

"I don't know, but I'm not plannin' to put it to the test. Let's get goin'." Don led the way to the police station's truck with Henry following close behind.

Sheriff Zen looked out his office window and watched them leave. He understood that this was his last good chance to stave off a rebellion in the town. He'd already been aware of grumblings and rumors from a few loyal residents who warned him that his tenure would come to a crashing halt if the case wasn't solved soon. People were afraid. They didn't dare venture past the town's boundary with the forest. They didn't want to be looking over their shoulders for the rest of their days. He sighed as he returned to his desk and murmured a little prayer for a successful mission.

No sooner had the deputies reached the forest surrounding Wren Falls than it began to rain. It was not a drizzle, not a moderate rain, not a brief period of precipitation—but a doggone downpour resembling a monsoon. The men hadn't brought much rain gear, just ponchos, and no tents they could shelter in. They were totally exposed. Their ammo and guns were soaked. As a last resort, they turned on the motor and then the heater, trying to dry out. They had their handguns in their side holsters, but all other weaponry was lying in the bed of the pickup, floating in about five inches of water. The deputies huddled together with the heater on full blast, eating some beef jerky with a chaser of water.

"Wish we'd brought some coffee," grumbled Don.

"Yeah, who knew the weather would do a one-eighty on us out here?" grumbled Henry.

"Shit," yelled Don. "We're off to a great start. How are we gonna kill this thing with waterlogged guns?" He threw up his hands in a gesture of disgust. "We might as well use water pistols," he complained.

"Calm down, Don. We got to keep our wits about us out here. This ain't no joke. We could lose our jobs if we don't wrap this one up," Henry explained.

"Yeah, I guess you're right," Don admitted. "Let's catch some shut-eye while we can. We sure can't track anything in these conditions." The two lawmen laid back in their seats and soon fell into a deep sleep, snoring in unison.

Henry, the lighter sleeper, noticed it first- an ungodly noise, like the cries of thirty or more dogs, all howling at once. *There ain't no pack of dogs or wolves with that many animals in it, no way. I must have imagined it.* The noise kept getting louder and, it seemed, closer. Don woke up.

"Geesh, what was that?" he asked his partner.

"Don't know. My imagination, I guess."

After a few more minutes of ferocious howling, Henry revised his opinion. "Guess not," he shivered, chilled from a combination of fear and the cold, driving rain.

The men looked at each other and then again at the rain, which hadn't shown any sign of slowing down.

"Holy cow," said Don "It's like the *Great Flood* out here. We could use an ark or at least a raft right about now. How are we gonna' get anything done? Sheriff's gonna have our heads if we come home empty-handed."

"Yeah," Henry agreed. He was only half paying attention to Don's words. The noise seemed to be closer, as if it was approaching their truck. "I think I'd better have a look around outside," he commented.

"Are you crazy?" Don looked at Henry incredulously. "You can't make out anything six inches in front of your face with this storm! What good would it do to go outside now? Wait a bit 'til it lets up."

"That noise we're hearing might be just what we're lookin' for. It's our chance to get a jump on whatever the thing is, that's making that awful sound. Then we can tie it up and drop it off in town," said Henry.

"Yeah, at the sheriff's feet!" laughed Don. "Can you just see his face?" He looked at his partner, and they both laughed heartily.

By now, they were giddy, and they had visions of being town heroes, celebrated publicly in the Wren Falls Town Square. Henry said to his partner, "I'll be back soon. I'm gonna' get that sucker." He pulled out his handgun and exited the truck. On a branch above his head, Henry noticed a large black bird staring at him. He paid it no mind. It was the last thing he noticed before Fate took him down.

Don had a silly grin on his face as he fantasized about bringing the beast to the sheriff's door. He was still grinning when a strangled voice screamed for help, as a deep growling and roaring shook the forest floor. Don slid over to the driver's side of the cab and peered out, looking for his friend. What he could barely make out would stay with him forever, the unrecognizable remains of a man he respected, who had two children and a loving wife waiting at home for him. In the last seconds of Don's sanity, a large snake head slammed into his driver's side window, transfixing Don with a malevolent stare, propelling his whole being into a deep state of shock. Ironically, he was the lucky one.

Chapter 19

The sheriff paced back and forth in his small office. He chomped on an unlit cigar, a habit he had given up three years ago and only resurrected when he was incredibly stressed. *Where the heck are they? It's been six hours since Henry and Don left here. They're my best trackers, and not a word from either of them? When I catch up with them, there's gonna' be hell to pay.* He plunked down into his comfy chair, and his mood shifted.

"What if something's happened to them and they need help?" he muttered under his breath. Scratching his stubble, he got up and called in his other deputies: three rookies and one ready for retirement—all in all, not too impressive a group.

"Boys," he began. "We need to form a search party for Don and Henry. I think they may be in trouble. We need to find them. This could be a dangerous mission. Anyone want to stay back and mind the fort instead?" Sheriff Zen was dismayed to notice everyone's hand go up.

"What's this? A bunch of lily-livered cowards on my team? You're all going and *that's that!*" he yelled. "Grab your gear and some extra firepower. Pack some vittles and your phones. We need to be able to communicate in them forests. Meet me outside in ten and take two squad cars. The truck's gone." The reluctant searchers were sure the sheriff meant business, and they hustled to get outside and into the cars in ten minutes, no more. When the sheriff slid into the driver's seat of car number one after locking the door to his office, they started their search in earnest.

Two hours later, after reaching the general forest area of Deepwoods Road, the officers filed out of the cars and began sloshing through the mud and the broken tree limbs in the direction of where they expected the truck would be located. The torrential rains had stopped. "Must've been some storm passed through here," one mumbled.

"Keep your mind focused on the job, Harris, and keep a sharp lookout for anything that seems unusual," said the sheriff, who had extraordinary hearing.

"Yes, sir," Harris answered.

After a prolonged period of traipsing through the brush and avoiding swampy terrain whenever possible, he spotted the pickup truck, partly visible in the distance. Harris shouted to the sheriff, who immediately instructed the group to fall in behind him and to draw their weapons.

"Don't make a sound, boys," the sheriff instructed. "We don't know what we'll find out here. It's awfully quiet." His spine stiffened as he came closer to the truck. He slowed his movements as the sweat poured down his face. He had a bad feeling.

Almost upon the police pickup, Harris tripped. He looked down and recognized the uniformed arm of one of the deputies. He turned around and retched. "What the heck?" asked the sheriff irritably. He spied the badly mauled body and joined Harris in heaving several times. By now, the others were aware of the situation and turned away.

Old Sam, ready for retirement, steered the younger men around the area and headed for the driver's side of the cab. He noticed Don sitting behind the wheel, not moving, not speaking, looking very much like a statue. He opened the door gently and tried to get Don's attention. "Don. Don, can you hear me? I've come to take you home, son. Back to your family. You just sit there, and I'll get you home," he said softly. He moved Don gently to the passenger side and strapped him in. Then he lifted Henry and his severed limb carefully into the back of the old truck. The sheriff approached the truck and thanked Old Sam for his efforts.

After a quick look around, no creature was visible in the vicinity, but they took some samples of the surroundings for examination at the lab, just in case. The men divided up into the squad cars and started the long trek home. Several of them cried for Don and Henry as they rode, but tears were also shed in relief that the rescuers were not the victims.

Sheriff Zen had a killer migraine. The partial dismemberment of one deputy and the incapacitation of another was a high price to pay for this investigation. *Maybe I'm getting too old for this game.* He hoped Don was just in a temporary state of shock and that he would be able to shed some light on what had happened in the forest. He visited Don in the neighboring town's hospital to get some information about his condition.

The news was not good. The doctors there said there was no way of knowing if Don would ever come out of his catatonic state. There was also little hope of Henry surviving. He was in an induced coma for the time being. The doctors reattached his arm and hoped against hope that Henry's physical wounds would begin to heal. The sheriff grieved for Henry and Don, his best detectives and good men besides. He trudged home, took a shower, ate something light, and went to bed, where he enjoyed a fitful sleep replete with ghastly nightmares.

In the morning, Sheriff Zen woke up with new resolve. He was helpless to heal his deputies, but he had to do something about this creature hiding in the woods. He needed to believe he was making progress in finding the predator that was stalking his community. He made up his mind to create a plan that would end these horrible events and restore the town to its former self, thereby saving his own reputation and the lives of his deputies.

Chapter 20

It had been a long time since Maeve and Sylvie paid a visit to Papa Will's house, and they were in the mood to do just that. School would be starting again soon, and they wanted to check out the spooky book of Celtic myths and legends, hoping to find a solution to their terrible problem with the beast. They also wanted to solve Alice's murder. Was there some kind of connection between the two? The girls arranged to meet the next day, and both were excited at the prospect. Sylvie had packed a picnic lunch for the two of them. They spread an old blanket on the living room floor—one that they'd found in an ancient trunk in Papa Will's bedroom.

"Someday, we'll have to explore the other rooms in this house. I'll bet there's lots of great stuff buried here."

"You bet!" agreed Maeve. "That old Celtic book that we look at all the time is just one example of something special hidden here."

"Let's go get it before we start eating," suggested Sylvie.

Maeve agreed, and the two of them went to the attic, and unburied the book from the pile of old photos. "I wonder who is in these pictures?" Maeve wondered. "There's no writing on the backs, and you can tell from the clothing and horse-drawn carriages that they lived a long time ago. It's a shame that they're lost to the rest of us. It would've been cool to know who they were."

Sylvie nodded and took Maeve's arm, pulling her to the staircase. "Come on, I'm hungry."

Maeve joined her descent, but added, "Someday, I'm going to start researching those people. There have to be records of them living here in Wren Falls, if that's actually where these photos were taken."

The two girls put the old book on the sofa, sat down on the living room floor, and began unwrapping their lunches. It appeared that Sylvie's dad had splurged and gone to the local bakery, purchasing croissants for the girls, which he stuffed with ham and cheese. He also packed a fruit salad and some iced tea. It was gourmet food for Maeve, and she gobbled it up with gusto.

"You are really lucky that your dad is so devoted to you, Sylvie. My dad doesn't even know I'm alive."

"Maybe he just can't show his feelings, Maeve. I can't believe he doesn't care about you."

"Believe it. Everything changed when my mother was murdered, and I don't expect it to get better, ever," Maeve commented sadly. "Let's change the subject. Now that we're done eating, we'll clean up and go read the book, *again*!" The two girls laughed and set about preparing to enjoy a good scare. It was one of their favorite activities, but Maeve had an ulterior motive as well. She planned to read more intently. Maeve hoped to find some important clues that would help her solve her mother's murder.

Sylvie and Maeve spread the huge book across their laps as they sat on the old, overstuffed sofa.

Maeve recalled, "Sylvie, we never got to read through the whole book. It's so big."

"You're right. Why don't we start where we left off?"

"Good idea," agreed Maeve. "I think we stopped at Morrigan, the Phantom Queen, foreteller of doom, caller of ravens, and shapeshifter extraordinaire," she added.

"You have quite a memory, Maeve, and an imagination to match," Sylvie laughed.

Maeve chuckled. "I believe the dear Queen often transformed herself into a black bird, perching herself near whoever was about to meet his or her terrible fate."

"Indeed. Let's keep going."

The girls turned the pages for another few hours and eventually came to the end of the book. The lopsided way it was perched on their laps caused it to slide off their laps and onto the carpet. It landed open to a specific page.

"Oh, my God!" Maeve blurted out. "It's the Questing Beast! It used to be my favorite of all the creatures in here, but now it just gives me chills to look at it. I need to read this carefully. It might help me find some clues to my mother's murder."

Sylvie picked up the heavy book and put it on a nearby table. She stared at it for a while and turned to Maeve.

"You know why this gives you chills? It's because all of these creatures are supposed to be legends or myths, but we've actually seen this monster up close, and we *have proof that* it's *real*!"

"Oh, God, Sylvie, you're right. We've actually been *chased* by this beast which was determined to attack us!" The two girls stared into the hypnotic eyes of the snake head, unable to turn away.

Suddenly, the front door swung open with such force, it banged against the wall and startled them. They screamed in unison until Maeve recognized her father storming into the living room.

"Aha! I expected to find you here. You got chores to do, young lady, and I need a good supper after a long, hard day. Who's this?" he pointed rudely at Sylvie.

"She's my friend, Sylvie." Maeve picked up the book and put it back on the table.

Sylvie never met James Newell, who was clearly drunk, and she could sense her friend's embarrassment. "I better go." She turned to Maeve, sympathy clouding her eyes. "I'll see you in school next week, Maeve."

Maeve looked sheepishly at her friend. "Sure. Bye," and turned to her father while Sylvie closed the front door as she left. "Why do you always have to ruin everything? She's my only friend, and now she probably won't want anything to do with me. You're always drunk, you don't work, and you leave me alone all the time. You don't care about me at all! I might as well be an orphan! You're just a good-for-nothin' lazy bum and I hate you!"

James, shocked at this outburst from his normally quiet and obedient daughter, was not too drunk to be unable to haul off and slap her hard on her right cheek, bringing stinging tears to her eyes.

"Now, you cut out this foolishness," as he threw the book on the floor, "and get yourself home to make my dinner! And take your damned dog outside. He's got his business to do. You'd best show me some respect before I kick you out of my house. How well will you do on your own? If your mother was alive, she'd be sick at your behavior!"

Maeve wanted to tell him to leave Alice out of this, but she didn't trust herself to stand up to her father any further. Once again, she wished to have a dad like Sylvie's.

Maeve walked slowly out of her grandpa's house, her head hanging low. As she passed her father in the doorway, he gave her a passing kick with his knee, just to show her who was boss.

Chapter 21

After her father's abhorrent behavior, Maeve needed to get away for a while. She called her Aunt Nelda and asked if she could stay for a few days.

"Anything wrong, dear?" asked Aunt Nelda.

"No more than usual," Maeve responded.

With an upturned arch of her eyebrows, Nelda asked no further questions and just replied, "Come for as long as you like, Maeve."

Grateful, Maeve packed an overnight bag and some food for Pooch and left a cryptic note for her father.

"Sleeping out. Don't look for Pooch or me. We'll be fine." She signed her name and left the house without a trace of regret.

Arriving at Nelda's, Maeve got a warm hug and a mug of cocoa with marshmallows for a greeting. She put her bag in the guest room, chatted with Nelda for a bit about superficial things, and then took Pooch outside for a walk. She was not far from Nelda's house when a loud hissing sound, and hoofbeats accosted her. With every passing minute, they seemed to be getting louder. Pooch must have sensed danger, too. He began to growl, and his ears flattened on his head as he bared his teeth. Not wasting a moment more, Maeve gave the command, "Pooch, Nelda's *now!*" and the dog ran full out with Maeve to Nelda's front door. A backward glance showed Maeve that the creature was gaining ground, and she barely made it into the house with her dog before the beast slammed into the closed door. Maeve locked the door and stepped away, shaking, the repeated blows of the beast smashing into the entrance as Nelda looked on in shock

"My goodness, Maeve! Whatever is making that horrific racket?" Nelda turned to Maeve with a puzzled look on her visage.

"It's the Questing Beast, Aunt Nelda. It's been stalking Sylvie and me for ages now. I don't know why, but it shows up out of nowhere—in the woods, in our dreams, on our way home from school, even on our camping trip with Miss Clouder! It's the creature that turned our bus over and caused some students and our teacher to wind up in the hospital!"

After a few minutes, an uneasy calm settled on the porch. Maeve looked out of the window, but the beast was not visible anywhere. Aunt Nelda and Maeve stood shaking behind the great throne chair in Nelda's living room. They hugged each other in relief.

"My poor dear, how terrifying!" comforted Aunt Nelda. "Have you told your father about this?"

"He wouldn't believe me," Maeve stood, her head hanging down, showing Nelda the toll the situation was taking on Maeve.

"Well, what about the sheriff? Surely, he would want to know about some creature that was stalking and attacking the people of his town?"

"I didn't tell him because I didn't want to panic the people of Wren Falls. I also didn't want them to think I was crazy. I hoped if I didn't talk about it, the beast would disappear."

"Is your plan working, Maeve?"

"It's not. I just don't know what to do anymore." Maeve looked defeated.

All of a sudden, the racket resumed, and Maeve began to tremble again. The beast's roar grew in intensity. The monster continued to pound on the door. A peek out of the casement window rewarded Nelda with a full view of the creature on its hind legs, pawing the door again with even greater ferocity. The hooves dug deep grooves into Nelda's magnificent mahogany entryway. But the most disturbing sight was the large snake head, complete with blazing red eyes, staring malevolently at Maeve's Aunt.

"Come, come," Aunt Nelda insisted. "This will not do. Oh, I can't stand that infernal racket outside." And with that, she dug into her pockets, pulled out a fistful of red dust, and threw it at the door.

The racket stopped. Maeve looked out a casement window on the side of the house.

The beast was gone.

"Oh, my gosh!" she yelled. "Is that all it takes to get rid of that monster? I should have told you about it long ago, and it would have disappeared from our lives!" Maeve was jubilant. *Maybe this will be the solution to getting rid of this creature.* She hoped against hope.

"Not so fast, my dear Maeve. That is just a temporary solution. The beast is only gone for the short run. It will be back."

By now, Maeve had regained her composure. Sadness replaced her agitation. "I wish this nightmare would end. I hate my life. My relationship with Pa is as bad as ever since Mom died. I miss her so, and this beast is threatening the people of Wren Falls, but I have no way to get rid of it."

"Now, now, Maeve. We will find a solution to this problem. Otherwise, what is my magic for? As for the rest of your life, you can always count on me for support, but you can't just expect good things to fall into your lap. You have to make your own good fortune," counseled Nelda. She steered Maeve into the kitchen with the great warm hearth, and the two of them sat across from each other, eating marzipan and chocolate croissants. The stress began seeping from Maeve's body like bathwater circling the drain. Aunt Nelda always had that effect on Maeve when she was agitated. She always seemed to comfort Maeve with the right words. Maeve often wished she could live with Nelda, instead of Pa, who was always out of sorts.

"Now," said Aunt Nelda. "Let's talk."

They had dinner—chicken cordon bleu, petit pois, and a strawberry shortcake dessert. They talked late into the night. Maeve went back to the beginning—how, after Papa Will died, she made regular visits to his house, sitting on his old swing, talking to his spirit. She went on to describe her first explorations of *The Encyclopedia of Celtic Lore* and her fascination with the creatures in it.

Later, she described her first encounter with Sylvie at school and the friendship that had developed over time. She detailed the many things they had in common and the one big thing they didn't—Sylvie had a loving, devoted dad, while Maeve had a distant, uncommunicative father who remained aloof since the death of her mother.

Maeve described her fear of the Questing Beast—how it had invaded her life, and later, Sylvie's life. She told Nelda about the camping experience, culminating in the beast's attack. Maeve also told Nelda about the sheriff's investigation and Annabeth Morgan's statement to him. She told Nelda that she had lied to the sheriff, not wanting to cause a town panic and hoping that the beast would eventually go away if she didn't betray its identity.

Nelda listened raptly, particularly when Maeve described the ghastly dreams she experienced. All of these details tumbled out of her in a stream of consciousness. It took hours for this conversation to end, and Maeve was clearly exhausted when she finished. Nelda stayed quiet through most of it, not wanting to interrupt the flow of Maeve's thoughts and emotions. The girl had bottled up so much, unable to confide in her one remaining relative, her father. Nelda made a mental note to talk to him soon. The situation between Maeve and her father was untenable. Nelda had promised Alice that she would look after Maeve if anything happened to her mother, and she believed she had not done a good enough job of it.

Maeve slept late the next morning. She dreamed about Grandpa Will. He had seemed so real. She was sure she could reach out and touch him. He was not his usual jovial self. Instead, he was scowling at her and shaking his head. She was aware she could form words asking him, "What is it, Papa?" (Against her will, she continued to raise questions—it was as though her grandpa was pulling her toward him with an invisible cord).

"What are you trying to tell me? Why are you angry?" He didn't answer Maeve, just kept shaking his head and moving closer to her. As he walked, Maeve could hear growling in the distance. Thundering hoof beats grew louder, and Maeve observed panic rising on her dream face. Just as the beast's head came into view, she woke up in a sweat.

For a moment, she didn't know where she was. When her heart's pounding slowed, she looked around and realized she was safe in Aunt Nelda's house. "I wonder what that dream meant?" she murmured. "Why was Papa so unfriendly towards me? Why wasn't he frightened by the beast approaching?" She spoke out loud, unconsciously. Still tired, Maeve told herself that she would discuss it with Nelda in the light of day, and meanwhile, she'd try to catch up on some much-needed rest. In a few minutes, she was relaxed and fast asleep.

At noon, Nelda came into the bedroom and drew open the drapes with some force.

"Come on, sleepyhead," she said loudly. "It's time for you to get up and start the day before the sun sets! I could use some help organizing my treasures from Hispaniola, and I've been waiting all morning!"

Maeve sat up slowly, rubbed the sleep from her eyes, and looked at her Aunt Nelda.

"How can you look so fresh and be energized at this time of the day?"

"This time of the day is lunchtime, my dear Maeve, even though you haven't even had breakfast yet," she laughed.

Maeve climbed out of the luxurious bed and began to dress behind an exotic Egyptian screen.

"Hurry up, girl," said Aunt Nelda. "I'm going downstairs to the kitchen to fix us a little something to eat," she said, and with that, she gave Maeve a casual wave of her hand and a radiant smile.

About fifteen minutes later, Maeve walked into the kitchen with the aromas of maple syrup and freshly baked muffins wafting through the room.

"Yum, I'm starving," she said and bolted to the closest seat she could reach at the table. In no time at all, she had gorged herself on a stack of six pancakes, two blueberry muffins, and three cups of cocoa. At the same time, Aunt Nelda had polished off an appetizing lunch of shrimp scampi and assorted fresh-baked breads.

"That was fantastic, Aunt Nelda!" *I wish I could eat like this every day.*

"I'm so glad you enjoyed our humble breakfast, Maeve. My lunch was quite delicious as well. Did you sleep well?"

"Not so much. I had a bad dream about my grandpa. He was angry with me and kept shaking his head. I don't know why he was upset with me, and I also don't know why he kept shaking his head at me. Does this make any sense to you?"

"Go on," urged Nelda.

"The really scary part was when I could sense the beast coming. The hoof beats kept getting louder and louder, the growling, too. Papa Will didn't seem to notice it at all. He didn't look scared or worried, not even when the snake head appeared in my dream.

"Then what happened?" probed Nelda.

"Nothing, I woke up in a sweat."

"If you are done eating, child, we can retire to the living room to continue this conversation as soon as I clean up these dishes," Nelda smiled reassuringly at Maeve.

"I can help," offered Maeve.

"No need, Maeve. I can take care of this in a second." Nelda reached into her pockets, pulled out two fistfuls of red dust, and threw it at the kitchen table and sink. In a matter of moments, the room looked like it had never been used. It was immaculate.

"Wow!" Maeve turned towards Nelda and exclaimed, "That was amazing!"

"Nothing to it, girl." Aunt Nelda indicated with her outstretched right hand that Maeve should proceed to the living room. And with that, Aunt Nelda began to answer some of Maeve's pressing questions, many of which she had been avoiding for quite some time.

Chapter 22

"Who was the good man who turned bad, Aunt Nelda? Do you know what my dream means? Why was Papa Will angry in the dream? How come he wasn't frightened when the beast arrived?" Maeve had a bunch of questions for her "aunt," and they poured out of her.

"Whoa! Wait a minute, Maeve." Nelda put out her hand with the stop motion hand signal of a school crossing guard. "I'll answer what I can, but you must realize that sometimes you may regret having an answer to a question. Sometimes, the answer can be so upsetting that you'll wish you never received it."

"I can handle it, Aunt Nelda, I've learned to be tough." *With a father like mine, I have to be.* "Please, can you explain my dream?"

"Dreams can mean many different things, Maeve. I need to consider it for a while before I interpret yours. Ask me something else in the meantime, and I'll puzzle that one out later."

"Okay," Maeve agreed. She wasn't happy about Nelda's response, but she would have to accept it for the time being. So, she pushed for the answer to another question that had been constantly on her mind. "Who was the good man that you said began to change and do terrible things, Aunt Nelda?"

Nelda sighed. "This is one of those questions that you may regret getting an answer to."

"No, I won't. I won't!" Maeve insisted, fairly bursting with curiosity. "Who was he?"

Nelda looked intently at Maeve, trying to assess the state of Maeve's emotional equilibrium. *Here goes,* she said to herself. *I hope she can handle the truth.*

"The person I was referring to," revealed Nelda, "was your grandfather, William Makepeace Newell."

There was dead silence in the room for several minutes. Suddenly, a blood-curdling scream came from Maeve as she gripped the arms of her chair in a stranglehold. The scream was followed by rapid gasps and heart-stopping outbursts of rage. Nelda kept her distance, waiting for Maeve to regain some of her composure, but it was not to be. Maeve looked at Nelda with such hatred that it was disturbing, to say the least.

"How could you say that about my grandfather?" she yelled. "You're lying! You must be lying You were his friend. I considered you mine as well! I hate you!" Maeve was shaking so hard she could barely get the words out.

"Desperate times call for desperate measures," murmured Aunt Nelda, and with that, she spun completely around three times in a counterclockwise direction. When she came to a complete stop, she was face to face with Maeve's puffy, red face. Only she was no longer Aunt Nelda. She was Goody Webster.

The shock of seeing Goody stopped Maeve in mid-scream. Goody held Maeve's arms in her own and quietly instructed her.

"Calm yourself, Maeve. All will be revealed, but not until you gain control of your emotions," responded Goody.

"What are you doing here?" Maeve's voice trembled as she tried to speak.

"Your grandfather and I have been close friends for many years, even millennia. I've come to tell you about him, so just sit tight and listen. Don't interrupt me or ask any questions until I finish my tale." Goody looked directly into Maeve's eyes.

Goody began. "I met your grandpa in Salem, Massachusetts, in the year 1689."

"1689? That's hundreds of years ago!"

"What did I say?" reminded Goody. "No more interruptions or I shall not continue."

"Sorry," mumbled Maeve.

"He was alone when he arrived," continued Goody, "and was doing odd jobs in Salem to sustain himself. I offered to take him in as a boarder, and he gladly accepted my offer. I was a Light Witch, making charms and potions on the side while baking bread and sweets for the townspeople. I used my magic to help people, and William and I became close friends. He alone had knowledge of my secrets.

"I had a book called *The Codex Demonicus* that was handed down to me by my Irish grandmother," Goody went on. "Salem was in an anti-witch frenzy at the time, and many good witches were killed after the terrible trials. Someone reported me to the town leaders, and on February 16, 1692, I had a hasty trial. Pronounced guilty, the elders sentenced me to death. Your grandpa visited me in my cell, and I gave him my grandmother's book for safekeeping. Will was the only one I trusted with it. He was a good and decent man.

"The book contained the secrets of all the evils in the world. I watched over it from the time I was a young witch and kept the monsters and creatures at bay for hundreds of years. I needed to have someone trustworthy continue my mission upon my death. Your grandfather accepted the assignment and the responsibility of keeping these evildoers in the book.

"As a reward for doing this task, he received the gift of longevity, not immortality, mind you, as he would eventually die as all humans do, but he would live many lifetimes before that day arrived. In exchange for this gift, William would never be able to have his own children. It would be too dangerous for them to live in the same house with this book of predators. Now, you may ask a question."

Maeve was tossing around the information she had just received in her brain, trying to make sense of it.

"I don't understand something, Goody. If Papa Will was not going to have any children, how did he have my pa?"

"An excellent question, my child. That brings us to the story of Miss Elizabeth Hathaway, whom your grandpa loved deeply. Now, listen very closely, for I shall only tell this part of the story once. It is too painful to tell repeatedly."

"Your grandpa was married to Elizabeth, who was much younger than he was. She was a talented gardener and horticulturalist. Your papa was very proud of her talents in those fields. He encouraged her to share her knowledge with other neighbors who would benefit from her tutelage.

"Elizabeth became very involved with one of the neighbors, and a child was the result of their relationship. Papa Will asked her about the unexpected pregnancy, and he accepted her explanation and her word that it was his child. Ultimately, he learned that the child was the neighbor's son, and he condemned his wife for her adultery. That child was raised by your grandpa and became your father."

Maeve was stunned. She couldn't believe what she was hearing. "Is Pa aware that he isn't Papa Will's real son?" she asked.

"No, he is not. Your grandpa never revealed the truth to him, and you must keep that information to yourself. It would break your father, and he is wounded enough by your mother's death."

"What did Grandpa do when he learned the truth?" Maeve asked.

"That betrayal caused your grandpa's descent into Evil. He was bent on punishing his wife, and eventually she paid the ultimate price." Goody concluded.

"You don't mean..."

Goody turned away from Maeve and said, "He arranged to have her killed."

Just as the Light Witch uttered these last words, Maeve fainted. She slid off her chair onto the floor, and none of Goody's attempts to revive her restored her to consciousness.

Goody sighed. She turned around three times in a clockwise direction and was gone. Aunt Nelda appeared in her place. Nelda dug into her pockets, withdrew two fistfuls of red dust, and threw it on Maeve's face and body. In seconds, Maeve came around and saw her aunt.

"When did you get here, Aunt Nelda? Where's Goody?"

"Goody is gone for now. She did what she had to do."

Maeve sat back in the chair. "She told me an incredible story, Aunt Nelda. Should I believe it?"

"Goody never lies, child. It's not in her DNA. Whatever she told you, it's the truth."

"My head is killing me. She told me some very disturbing information about my grandpa, and I have a massive headache."

"Come into the kitchen, Maeve, and have some tea and croissants. It will cure what ails you," offered Nelda.

"I don't think I'll ever be able to see my grandpa in the same light again," Maeve said sadly. "It's so hard for me to believe that this gentleman who read me stories when I was young, who regaled the townspeople with his comical anecdotes and tales, and who was so kind to me when my mother died...how could he be capable of such savagery?"

"Rage can make people do terrible things, Maeve."

"How did he do it, kill his wife, I mean?"

"I think you've had enough for today, Maeve. You need time to adjust to what you have learned from Goody," Nelda explained. "We can talk about that some other time. Besides, what difference does it make? The end result is the same—tragic."

"I suppose you're right, Aunt Nelda," admitted Maeve quietly. "I am exhausted. I think I'll go take a nap for a little while."

"And when you awaken, Maeve, you'll eat something nourishing. I'll take Pooch out for a walk, and we'll talk later."

Maeve went to the guest room while Nelda wrestled with her conscience in the living room. She didn't really want to get into the gory details of Elizabeth Hathaway's demise with Maeve. She didn't know how far to go in Papa Will's story. Maeve nearly had a breakdown when Nelda told her that Papa Will was the good man who transformed into an evildoer. She hoped she could put Maeve off, for a while, and distract her with stories about Alice or a discussion of Maeve's father/daughter relationship. Nelda sighed. *This is getting too complicated.* She was also running out of red dust and would have to replenish her supply soon. She expected it would be an indispensable tool in future encounters.

Maeve rejoined Nelda in the dining room. In a moment, Nelda magically produced a lovely spread of Maeve's favorite foods with mouth-watering desserts to match.

"I'm starving!" Maeve announced. "Thanks so much for this incredible meal, Aunt Nelda!"

"You're welcome, my dear. Let's eat and chat about only positive things, my child."

So, they tucked hungrily into their repast and chatted about Sylvie, her father, and the friendship that had grown between the girls.

"I'm so pleased that you have made a good friend, Maeve. That is essential in life."

"Especially *my* life," commented Maeve.

"Tsk! Tsk! Only pleasant topics at lunch, Maeve! It helps digestion," concluded Nelda.

"Sorry. I think I need to go home after lunch, Aunt Nelda. Pa must be wondering where I am. He's probably missing his Cinderella," she added with a wry expression on her face.

Ignoring that comment, Nelda agreed and reminded Maeve that if she ever needed her, she should never hesitate to call on her. They said their goodbyes, and Nelda watched from her window as Maeve and Pooch made their way home, the long way.

Maeve was in no hurry to return home. She could do without her father's temper tantrums and his whiskey binges. They never had any conversation other than his orders for her and his complaints about the way she did her chores. It was getting tiresome, and she wished for a family life that approached normalcy. *That's one dream that will probably never come true,* she sighed. *I guess I'm lucky to have Aunt Nelda in my life. She's such an extraordinary person.*

Maeve started for home, keeping a watchful eye on the woods in front of her. She had no desire to experience a deadly confrontation with the Questing Beast today or any other day.

"About damned time you came home," growled James Newell when Maeve returned home. "Where the hell have you been?" he demanded as Maeve stepped through the doorway. "I can't fix my own meals, and you know I can't even boil water," he added.

"I was at Aunt Nelda's," said Maeve. "We had some things to discuss. I didn't think you'd miss me much while I was gone."

"Well, you were wrong about that, Missy. No man should have to clean his own house, make his own meals," he complained. "So, I didn't do any cleaning, and I ate my meals down at the bar."

"What a surprise," Maeve muttered.

"What'd you say, girl? "Don't you be bad-mouthin' me under your breath. You'd best remember what I said about showin' some respect if you're gonna' stay in this here house."

"Yes, Pa," Maeve answered, thinking to herself, *as if I'd want to stay in this house if I had any other choice.* "I'll just take Pooch out for a short walk, and then I'll start making you some dinner."

"That's more like it," Pa grunted at his daughter as he watched her leave with Pooch. "Worthless, good-for-nothin' girl. I wish I had a son instead, like my pa."

Maeve couldn't wait to get back to school and spend some precious time with Sylvie. They had Miss Clouder again this year, since she always taught the older kids, so it wasn't unusual to have her for several school years. "*Good thing I like her*," Maeve said to herself.

The next day, Maeve met up with her friend at the fork in the road. They chattered like magpies until they got to the school door. The girls agreed to meet for lunch under their favorite tree to catch up on any news left over from the summer.

At lunch, Sylvie mentioned a brief trip to visit her Nana in Kentucky. She described the beautiful horse farms in the area and Nana's fabulous cooking.

"I think I must have gained ten pounds down there," she laughed. My dad tries his best, but his cooking can't hold a candle to Nana Amelia's." Her tone of voice suddenly switched to a more serious one. "We visited my mom and my brother while we were there. I mean, we visited their graves.

I talked to them. It was sad, but it made me feel better," she added. "I miss them so."

Eager to distract Sylvie, Maeve told her about her dream. She described the peculiar behavior of Papa Will and her stay at Aunt Nelda's. She raised the question that had plagued her at Nelda's house. "What does the dream mean?" But Sylvie was at a loss. Maeve also described her welcome home reception from her pa.

"Things haven't improved in that area, have they?" asked Sylvie sympathetically.

"No," said Maeve, "and I doubt they ever will. I'm so glad we're finally having a chance to talk, Sylvie. I've missed our time together this summer."

"Me, too," said Sylvie. "Uh, oh, look at the time. We'd better clean up our mess and get back to the classroom. How about if we meet at the Historical Society library tomorrow after school?" she suggested.

"Sounds like a plan," said Maeve. The two friends rushed to clean up the remains of their lunches and ran back into the classroom. As much as they liked Miss Clouder, they were rule followers at heart.

Chapter 23

Sheriff Zen made frequent trips to the hospital to check on Don's progress on the Psych Ward and Henry's in the ICU. No change in Henry's condition, but today, Don seemed happy to see the sheriff. He was sitting up in a chair, eating his lunch, when the sheriff entered his room. It looked as if Don would be discharged soon and be able to resume his normal life. No doubt about it, he seemed much better, and the sheriff was hopeful that Don would be able to supply some vital details about the day he and Henry went looking for the creature. The stalemated investigation frustrated the sheriff to no end. He was determined to solve the mystery of what was plaguing the residents of Wren Falls.

"Hey there, Sheriff! Good to see ya!" Don called to him.

"Howdy, Don," answered the sheriff. "Glad to see you're on the mend."

"Yes, I'm feelin' much better, sir. I think I'll be outta here in no time."

"Good to hear, Don. Good to hear," responded the sheriff. "I wonder if I could ask you a few questions about the day you and Henry went to investigate in the forest?"

Don's expression went from pleasant to a plain stare to a state of shock—a look of horror stamped on his face. The sheriff shifted uncomfortably in his seat.

"Don, Don, are you okay?" Zen asked in a soft voice.

Don's answer came in a high-pitched, blood-curdling scream that punctured the sheriff's eardrums and seemed to go on forever.

"Doctor!" yelled the sheriff. "I need a doctor right away, *now*!" yelled Zen to anyone who would listen. He stuck his head into the hall outside Don's room and screamed for help until a team of first responders raced into the room and ushered him out.

"You need to leave, sir. We'll take care of him. Leave now!"

The sheriff raced out of the hospital, into his police car, and did something he never did. He cried. He cried for a good forty minutes until he could come back to himself enough to engage the engine of the car and drive slowly back to his station house.

When Zen arrived at the police station, he remained in the car. He thought about his two wounded deputies—one physically injured, the other mentally incapacitated. He desperately needed to solve this case. He owed their families that much.

Zen was wracked with guilt because, not knowing what evil lurked in the woods, he sent them into danger without backup. *How could I have known what they would be facing?* He asked himself. Still, it was an impulsive decision, heavily influenced by political factors, and one which he deeply regretted.

The sheriff stepped out of the station car and marched purposefully into the locker room to find his unit.

"On your feet, men! We're forming a search party. We're going to find that murdering beast and put an end to it, if it's the last thing we do! We will rid this town of that evil creature and avenge Don and Henry! It's the least we can do for our fellow officers. Now, everyone outside in ten—fully armed!"

The men scurried to get ready. They could tell the sheriff was in no mood for delays or excuses. The look on his face told them everything they needed to know. The sheriff meant business! All of them were ready, their weapons fully loaded, in not a second more than seven minutes!

The girls were finally back in their favorite place—the library at the Historical Society. "Let's go back to the file on Elizabeth Hathaway," suggested Sylvie. The thought of reviewing the details of Elizabeth's death made Maeve nauseous. Now that she was aware that her grandpa was implicated in Elizabeth's death, she was not so eager to learn more about it. She was afraid of how ugly the case might be and what further information she might acquire.

"I don't know, Sylvie," Maeve said. "I think we pretty much exhausted that one."

"How can you say that, Maeve? We don't know who or what killed her, and the case is still unsolved," Sylvie added.

"Yeah," said Maeve, "but there don't seem to be any more clues in these articles." She tried to change the subject, which was making her uncomfortable. She wasn't sure how much longer she could keep the truth from her friend. She would have to tell her eventually that her grandpa was responsible, but it didn't have to be today. What would Sylvie think of her if she learned that Maeve's grandpa was a murderer in addition to the fact that her father was a drunken bum?"

"Let's just check out a few of these other cases, okay? We can always go back to this one another day. What about the recent attack on the sheriff's deputies? That case isn't solved either."

"Yeah, that might be interesting," agreed Sylvie. "Let's take a stab at that one."

Maeve shuddered at the use of the word 'stab' and nodded in acquiescence.

"Are you cold, Maeve?".

"Just a bit. I'll put my sweater on,".

They spent the rest of the day poring over recent news accounts of one deputy's near-death mauling and the other's psychotic break.

"This case sounds a lot like Elizabeth Newell's, Maeve, even though it's so many years later"

Maeve nodded silently. Suddenly, she couldn't wait to leave the library.

"Why don't we go get a snack at Little Piggy's?" suggested Maeve.

"Good idea. I'm hungry anyway," answered Sylvie. They packed up their books and strode over to their favorite hangout, and Maeve sighed a deep sigh of relief.

That night, Maeve tossed and turned in her bed. When she finally fell asleep, the image of her grandpa floated into her unconscious mind. This time, he was smiling at her, but the smile was ungodly. His teeth were yellow sharpened fangs, and blood dripped from each of them. He had a sardonic grin on his pale gray face as he pointed the gnarled, spindly right index finger at Maeve. His nails were black and blue, and there were deep hollows under his eye sockets. Maeve couldn't look away from the prominent veins crisscrossing his face, giving him the look of a 3D monster. He mouthed the word *"you,"* over and over again as he pointed at her.

Maeve shook uncontrollably. She called out for her father, but no one came. Her grandpa laughed wickedly, seeing that no one was responding to Maeve's distress call. He then moved his index finger from right to left in a warning motion and moved closer to her bed. He was enshrouded in a long black cloak.

At that precise moment, Pooch jumped up on the bed, bared his teeth, and growled at the vision, loudly enough to wake Maeve out of her nightmare. She rolled onto her side and tried desperately to catch her breath and calm down.

"What's all the racket in here?" yelled her father as he barged into her room.

"I was having a nightmare, Dad. Where were you? I called out to you for help."

"I was trying to get in some shut-eye, Maeve, but you made *that* impossible. You're too old for nightmares, girl. Grow up and stop acting like a baby," he added. "Goddamn it!" James Newell shouted. "I need this crap like I need a second head."

He slammed the door so hard that the walls shook.

Maeve held Pooch for a while, petted him, and thanked him for her rescue. The two of them curled up next to each other and lay awake for the rest of the night.

Chapter 24

About a week after Maeve's disturbing dream, Sylvie surprised her with an invitation for a sleepover.

"I'd love to come!" Maeve responded. Life at home with her father was becoming more and more unbearable. A sleepover at Sylvie's was just the right medicine for what ailed her. Sylvie grinned and said she was glad they'd have some time to spend together without responsibilities and chores getting in the way. Her dad supported her friendship with Maeve. He even allowed her to pass on taking out the garbage and helping to clean the house under special circumstances. A sleepover was just the kind of special circumstance that would qualify.

When Maeve got home from school, she found her father waiting for her. It was unusual for him to be home and sober during the afternoon. Maeve's guard went up immediately, wondering what he was after.

"I have to go out of town, Maeve," he said. "There's some business I have to take care of concernin' your grandpa's house. I'll be away for three days, and need you to look after things here durin' that time. You're old enough to stay on your own, and the place better be clean and the laundry done when I get home."

"When are you going, Dad?"

"Now."

He didn't say anything endearing to Maeve, just that he would leave thirty dollars on the kitchen table for her to buy food for her and Pooch. He picked up his knapsack, threw a "So long" over his shoulder to his daughter, and walked out the front door.

Maeve was stunned. Her feelings were a mixture of relief that he was leaving for a few days and curiosity about what he was planning for Grandpa's house. She had never been totally alone in her house for that long, which made her a bit nervous as well. Sylvie's sleepover was the next weekend, so the amount of time she would be spending with her father would be limited for the next week. It made her sad to realize that the absence of contact with him didn't even faze her. She wouldn't miss him, and that was an unhappy realization, too.

"It's just you and me, Pooch," she said to her dog as she poured out some food for him and set it on the floor. The rest of Sunday passed uneventfully.

"I wonder who Dad is going to see?" she said to the dog as if he would understand her. She'd gotten used to using him as a sounding board with no one else in the house to talk to. Her father was seldom around, and when he was, he wasn't interested in anything she had to say. He was preoccupied with his own needs and nothing more.

The next two days passed quickly, between school, homework, cleaning the house, and doing the laundry. She wasn't going to give her father anything to complain about. She'd had enough of his temper to last a year, and she wanted to be in a good frame of mind when she went to Sylvie's. Maeve didn't want anything to ruin that planned visit. Thinking about it actually put a smile on Maeve's face as she thought about the activities they would do together. She was in a fine mood as she swept the floors, when suddenly, the phone rang.

It was Aunt Nelda on the phone.

"Hello, Maeve. I wonder if you would like to come visit for the day. I've been thinking about your dream and have some ideas about it."

"That would be great, Aunt Nelda. I've had a second dream since then, which was even scarier, but we can talk about it later. What time should I come?"

"Any time this afternoon will be fine. Of course, if you would like to sleep here tonight, bring a change of clothes and your books for school. Pooch is always welcome," Aunt Nelda replied.

"I'll come as soon as the laundry is finished," Maeve eagerly agreed. After she hung up the phone, Maeve started the last wash, folded the earlier wash in the dryer, and sorted it into the proper drawers. She prepared an overnight bag and finished any last minute cleaning chores that remained. Finally, Maeve began her trek to Nelda's with Pooch—the long way, of course.

It had been a while since Maeve had seen the Questing Beast, and she hoped against hope that it had left the area. She racked her brain for ways to get rid of it, haunted by the fact that others could be injured or worse by it. Her walk to Nelda's was uneventful. However, she wasn't in Nelda's home more than five minutes before she began to notice growling outside the door.

"What in the world is that awful noise?" asked Nelda impatiently.

"I hope it's not what I think it is," Maeve replied. She looked at Pooch, who was already baring his teeth and whose ears were flattened back on his head.

"Uh oh," whispered Maeve. "I think we've got a very unwelcome visitor."

Aunt Nelda peeked out a side casement window and came face to face with a large, red-eyed snake head that was staring intently at her. "Oh, my," Nelda mumbled. "I fear we have a problem, Maeve."

Nelda ran upstairs to a bedroom directly above the beast and opened the window. Fortunately, she had replenished her supply of red dust only the previous week, so she dug into her pockets and grabbed two fistfuls of it. In one swift motion, Nelda threw the dust down on the beast's head. Maeve watched the red particles float down to the snake's skull, and, as quickly as the beast appeared, it disappeared. Maeve exhaled.

"Thank God for that magic dust."

"As I told you before, Maeve, it is not a permanent solution, just a temporary one."

"Right, Aunt Nelda, but still, it's great to have in an emergency. Why does that thing keep showing up wherever I go?"

"I think the answer to that is intertwined with your dreams, Maeve," Nelda offered. "The explanation may be hard for you to accept. This whole affair is complicated for a young girl like yourself to comprehend."

"I'm willing to try, Aunt Nelda."

"Very well, Maeve. Let's go into the living room, get comfortable, and we'll begin." The two, comfortable in overstuffed Queen Anne armchairs, settled themselves in for a difficult, and possibly disturbing, discussion.

"Last we spoke, child, we discussed the fact that your grandpa was the good man who turned evildoer. This was very hard for you to accept, and I needed to call upon Goody to help you comprehend the situation. We also revealed that your grandpa was responsible for his wife, Elizabeth's, death. I realize that day was very traumatic for you. In addition, the story of Elizabeth's betrayal informed you of the fact that your father was not Papa Will's son, but the result of the adulterous liaison between Elizabeth and her neighbor," summarized Nelda.

"Yes," said Maeve. "It was a very painful and confusing conversation for me. I still haven't shared this information with Sylvie, and it's hard to keep it from her since we share everything else."

"I see, Maeve," said Nelda. "Why exactly have you kept it from her?"

"Aunt Nelda, Sylvie's seen Pa at his worst. She already knows he's a drunk and verbally abusive to me. What would she think if she learned my grandpa was a murderer? She comes from a normal family. How could she understand all this?"

"I think, Maeve, if she's as caring as you say she is, she won't judge you by your relatives. She knows *you* and she won't blame you for the actions of your family members. Anyway, you'll have to tell her sooner or later. It's just too much to hide. It would become a wall between the two of you, and you don't want that," insisted Nelda.

"No, I don't.".

"Okay, well, think about it. Let's talk about the dream. The one with your grandpa who was scowling at you and saying 'No' over and over again. What do you think it means, Maeve?"

"I've been wracking my brain for weeks now and still have no idea."

"Well," Nelda explained, "I think it was your grandpa's way of warning you off your investigation of the cold cases. I think he didn't want you to discover his part in Elizabeth's death, nor that your father was not his son. In addition, the fact that he was not alarmed when the beast showed up says to me that he is entirely comfortable with the creature—that he has some kind of relationship with it. That makes him an incredibly dangerous spirit, Maeve. He is not the kindly, funny Papa Will that you remember, but rather an evil presence that does not wish you well. You'd best remember that."

Maeve looked at Nelda, fear emanating from her face. "Are you saying, Aunt Nelda, that I need to be afraid of his spirit? That the beast is stalking me because Papa Will is directing it to?"

"I'm saying that is very likely, Maeve, and what other information is he trying to keep from you? There may be much more to these cold cases than the police know. How did Elizabeth die? Is there a connection between your grandpa, the beast, and her death?" questioned Nelda.

Maeve shuddered. "This is really scary, Aunt Nelda. Maybe it's too dangerous for Sylvie to be my friend and be seen with me. What should I do?"

"I have no idea, Maeve. No idea at all."

To distract Maeve from thinking constantly about their recent conversation, Aunt Nelda introduced her to the board game, Backgammon. Maeve was aware of the game but never played it, so the hours passed quickly until it was time for supper.

"I *am* hungry, Aunt Nelda, but I didn't realize how long we've been playing," Maeve admitted.

"Yes," admitted Nelda with a sly grin on her face. "You are quite the competitor, Maeve. It didn't take you very long to learn the game and beat me!"

"It was really fun," remarked Maeve, "and it was a good break from the dark thoughts that were spinning around in my brain this afternoon."

They left the living room, and with a flick of Nelda's wrist in a back-handed motion, the game put itself back into the box and took its proper place on the correct shelf.

"I believe we have quite a lovely dinner prepared for us, Maeve. Wait 'til you see!"

"Yum! I can't wait. I'm starving!"

As they walked into the dining room, Maeve noticed that the silverware was gold and there was a matching gold rim around each white plate. There were crystal goblets at each setting and a Waterford crystal pitcher of ice water on the table. In the center of the table was a perfectly cooked quail accompanied by various side dishes and salads. Maeve was breathless.

"Oh, my, Aunt Nelda, the table is magnificent, and the food looks amazing," gushed Maeve.

"Well, don't just stand there, girl, make yourself comfortable and fix yourself a plate." Maeve pulled out an overstuffed dining room chair and got right down to business. She ate until she couldn't fit another morsel in her belly. When she was done, a tray of fabulous desserts appeared at the end of the table with tortes, pies, miniature cookies, a chocolate strawberry shortcake, and next to it, a fondue station for dipping fruits in dark chocolate. Aunt Nelda had to explain to Maeve how the fondue station worked—she had never seen one before, but she adapted to it quickly!

When dinner was over, Maeve excused herself and prepared for an early bedtime. She was completely drained from the day and needed a good night's sleep. Nelda kissed her goodnight and arranged for the cleanup in the dining room. A few fistfuls of red dust did the trick, and Nelda sat down in a tufted club chair in the living room to read. She could not focus on her book. Her mind kept going to the afternoon's discussion.

Nelda was aware what kind of man Will *used to be* and *what he had become*. She was also aware that his character completely changed once he began wreaking vengeance on the people he believed had been disloyal to him. The new Will was unrecognizable from the man she worked with when she was a Light Witch in Salem. *How far would he go? Would he actually destroy his own granddaughter in his lust for revenge and his desire to save his reputation in Wren Falls?* These thoughts tormented Nelda throughout the night. She had to protect Maeve, but how? She couldn't be with her every minute of every day.

She also worried about Sylvie. The girls were very close, and it would break Maeve psychologically if anything happened to her. The last thing she wanted was for Maeve to live with guilt the rest of her life if Sylvie was collateral damage in Maeve's story. Nelda sighed and tried to sleep, but her thoughts kept her awake past midnight. When she arose in the morning, she was not the ebullient, positive person that Maeve expected.

"Is anything wrong, Aunt Nelda?"

"No child. I was just overstimulated from our busy day yesterday. I couldn't unwind enough to get a good night's sleep," admitted Nelda. She didn't want to add to Maeve's concerns, so she hurried her into the kitchen for breakfast with Pooch and then sent her on her way to school. Nelda said she would bring Pooch home sometime during the day, and Maeve was eager to reconnect with Sylvie in class to tell her about her stay at Nelda's. She was sure it was going to be a wonderful day.

She was wrong.

Chapter 25

Maeve and Sylvie were delighted to be together again. "I have lots to tell you, Sylvie!"

"Why don't you stop by my house? My dad's away, and we could have the house to ourselves until Aunt Nelda comes by to return Pooch."

"Sure," said Sylvie. "I don't think my dad would mind. I'll just leave him a note, and then we can walk together to your place."

"Great," Maeve replied. "We'll go straight from school," and the two turned their attention back to Miss Clouder's lesson on World History.

After school, the two friends packed up their books and supplies and set out for Sylvie's place. It was not long before they reached her house, where she dropped off her books in her bedroom. She sat down to write her dad a note and said to Maeve, "I think there's some mint chocolate chip ice cream in the fridge. That's your favorite, so why not have some before we go to your place?"

Maeve, who was always hungry, helped herself to a heaping bowl of ice cream and greedily wolfed it down. "That was terrific, Sylvie," she exclaimed. "You'd better have some yourself before I eat it all!" Sylvie smiled broadly and helped herself to a generous portion as well.

"What a great day this is turning out to be!"

Sylvie nodded in agreement since she had a mouthful of ice cream and was taught never to speak with her mouth full.

The girls headed for Maeve's house. When they arrived, Maeve noticed how bare the house looked compared to Nelda's and Sylvie's. It seemed even emptier without Pooch or her father there. On the other hand, she enjoyed a sense of liberation—being on her own with certain responsibilities, almost as if the house belonged to her.

"Come into the living room, Sylvie. I have so much to fill you in on."

"Okay, shoot. I'm all ears."

Maeve launched into the tale of Elizabeth's death. She filled in all the details that Nelda had supplied. The most disturbing aspect of the story came when Maeve explained why Elizabeth was killed and by whom.

"You mean, you mean your grandpa killed Elizabeth?" Sylvie asked incredulously.

"Yes, Sylvie. He viewed her adultery as a massive betrayal and could think only of getting his revenge."

"What about his son?"

"Oh, he loved him, but his son was really Elizabeth's lover's son. Will raised him as his own and never told him that they were not blood relations.

Sylvie's eyes widened. "You mean that your father isn't aware that he isn't Papa Will's son?"

"That's right," admitted Maeve.

"Isn't aware of what? What don't I know, Maeve?" demanded her father as he entered the living room at that moment. The girls exchanged looks.

Uncomfortable with the unexpected situation, Sylvie collected her things and turned to Maeve. "I'd better go. You need to have a private conversation with your dad."

"Don't go, Sylvie, please," begged Maeve. "What are you doing here, Dad? You weren't due back until tomorrow," she said forlornly.

"My meeting ended early. Don't change the subject," he insisted. "What don't I know?"

The explosion was coming. "Maybe you'd better go home, Sylvie. I'll call you later."

"Talk later," Sylvie replied and scurried out the door, sensing the charged atmosphere in the house. On her way home, Sylvie thought about the relationship between Maeve and her father. In her mind, she drew a comparison between her own relationship with her father and Maeve's with hers. Both men were widowers and single parents. Her father treated her like treasure. He was attentive, affectionate, a bit strict sometimes, but definitely caring and loving. Maeve's father treated her like Cinderella. There was no affection that Sylvie perceived, no attention or demonstration of concern. And it didn't seem like it would ever get better.

How sad for Maeve. If anything happened to Aunt Nelda, Maeve would have no one in her life she could count on. It almost made Sylvie cry, but then she remembered, *"except me!"* The concept brought a smile to Sylvie's face, and she recognized she would always be there to support Maeve through anything. *That's what friends are for*, she thought to herself as she entered her house, oblivious to the monster lurking a quarter mile away, behind a cluster of elm trees.

"You'd better sit down, Dad," Maeve instructed him, anticipating that this was not going to go well.

"I don't need to sit down, Maeve. I need some straight talk. *Now*."

Maeve took a deep breath, sat down on the threadbare couch, and began. "This will be hard for you to hear, Pa. Just listen 'til I'm through. I completely trust this information and its source. I've been working for several months in the Historical Society library, trying to solve some of the town's cold cases."

"With your little friend, I suppose?" sneered her father.

"With Sylvie, yes," Maeve replied. "We've actually made some good progress. We were looking into the case of Elizabeth Newell, nee Hathaway, who died mysteriously."

"You mean my mother," said James Newell.

"Well, that's where it gets complicated," said Maeve. "She was your mother, but Papa Will wasn't your real father."

"What?" yelled Pa. "Who filled your head with that garbage?"

Maeve related the story of Elizabeth's affair, Papa Will's rage at her betrayal, and her murder. She made sure to explain that Papa Will raised James Newell as his beloved son, but they did not share the same bloodline.

"Have you lost your mind, Maeve?" her father asked.

"No, Sir. Papa Will killed your mother. He was not your father, nor was he my blood grandfather," she added.

"You have gone off the deep end, Maeve. You are truly a nutcase. I can't believe what I'm hearing. Who have you discussed this with, besides Sylvie?" he asked, his face about two inches away from hers, anger flooding it with color.

"Me," came a voice from the front hall, followed by familiar barking.

Maeve ran to Pooch and embraced him. Then she ran up to Aunt Nelda, threw her arms around Nelda's waist. "Thank goodness you are here, Aunt Nelda! Pa doesn't believe me and he's furious," she said tearfully.

"Your daughter is completely correct, James. I have known William for more years than I care to remember, and I can tell you everything Maeve said is accurate. Betrayal is his trigger, and he is guilty of vicious crimes because of it."

James collapsed into his old club chair, put his head in his hands, and said, "My head is spinning. Why have you never told me this, Nelda?"

"There is much more to tell, James. After Alice's death, you were in no condition to listen to any of it. If you hadn't walked in here unexpectedly, I wouldn't have told you anything, and I'm sure Maeve wouldn't have either. You've been an absentee father to your own child. You've been unkind to her and distant. She has suffered greatly from your lack of attention and affection."

The figure slumped in the chair and began to cry. The body, racked with sobs, seemed to be expelling a great sadness that had paralyzed his emotions for years. Maeve didn't recognize her father. She didn't realize he had that depth of feeling within him. This was a side of Pa that was hidden for years.

Maeve went over to him and put her hand on his shoulder in a gesture of empathy. Her father reached up and took her hand in his.

"I'm so sorry, Maeve. When your ma died, I couldn't think about anything but my own feelings. Her murder filled me with rage. I just couldn't focus on you. It was like you were invisible or somethin'," he said to her.

"Yes," whispered Maeve, feeling like some wall between them was gradually coming down brick by brick. She was sad for her father, but part of her was excited that this could be a new beginning for them.

"There is much more to discuss," Nelda broke in, "but we will leave that for another day."

Just then, the three of them heard a persistent growling and hissing outside the living room windows.

"Oh, no!" yelled Maeve. "It's back!"

"What's back?" asked her father.

"The Questing Beast, James," said Nelda. "Take a good look outside and see what your daughter has been grappling with for the better part of this year."

James got up quickly and ran to the windows. He found himself eye to eye with the snake's head, its fangs dripping with saliva, and a brief look at the features of other assorted animals that make up the creature.

"Oh, my God!" he exclaimed.

"Yes, James. That is the beast that killed your mother on Papa Will's order! And what's more, it is also the murderer of your dear Alice, also on Will's orders!" Nelda raged.

"Oh, no! You can't mean that, Aunt Nelda!" Maeve's head began to spin.

In the next moment, Maeve was lifted onto the couch by her father's strong arms as she descended into darkness. While Maeve was unconscious, Nelda dispatched the beast with her magical red dust.

"How did you learn to do that?" asked James.

"You'd be surprised what I can do, James, but that's a conversation for another day." She sat down across from him and filled him in on everything that Maeve had been dealing with the past year while he was in an alcoholic haze.

"Oh, no!" he moaned. "I haven't been there for her when she really needed me."

"Very true," said Nelda, "but it's never too late to start." She gave him a penetrating stare. "Are you willing to become a real father to her now?"

He nodded, watching over Maeve as she slowly began to come back from her faint.

"You must have many questions, James. I think we've discussed enough for today, and it will take time to absorb such traumatic information. I will leave you two for now, but I will be back to check on how you are doing," Nelda said.

"Thank you, Nelda," said James, "for taking care of Maeve when I couldn't, and for being a shoulder for her to lean on when she needed one."

"You are most welcome," she answered. "Maybe there's hope for you, after all."

Nelda walked gracefully to the door after checking the view from the windows and disappeared down the road leading to her home.

That afternoon, Maeve and her father had their first real conversation since Alice's burial. Owing to the important meeting he had just come from, he was sober for the first time since Alice died, and they were able to clear the air about many things. Maeve began by outlining for James what she had learned from Nelda. She included her research with Sylvie, regarding the unsolved cases of Elizabeth, and now it appeared, her mother. She told James Newell about *The Codex Demonicus* that belonged to her grandfather. She described the times she had spent with Will when he regaled her with stories relating to these mythological creatures, retold in *The Encyclopedia of Celtic Lore*. Maeve explained the closeness she had experienced with her grandpa, while her father was unapproachable. James Newell listened quietly, remorse fueling his conflicted emotions.

Maeve shared her feelings of loneliness with her father. Having no one at home to offer support, Maeve turned to Aunt Nelda, the closest thing to a sister for Alice and a substitute mother figure for Maeve.

"I've depended on her a lot, Dad," she said. "Until Sylvie moved in, I didn't even have a close friend that I could turn to when I needed comfort or understanding. I was totally alone. You were never home, and when you were, well...." Her voice drifted off.

"I'm real sorry, Maeve," he responded. "I have a lot to make up to you."

"I'm just glad we have this chance to reconnect." Maeve lowered her voice. "I never thought it would happen."

"I promise, Maeve," said her dad, "I'm turnin' over a new leaf. We'll throw out all the whiskey in the house, and I'll smash up the still. I want to be a father to my girl." He gave her a self-conscious smile.

Maeve responded in kind and continued her narration. She told him about the Questing Beast, which stalked the two girls, particularly Maeve, for the past year. She described the frightening experience at the campgrounds and the vicious attack on Deputy Henry and Deputy Don, which had significant similarities to the maulings of Elizabeth and Alice. She related the harrowing dreams she had about her grandpa, which were getting scarier by the minute, and she detailed how Pooch had saved her several times from the beast.

James Newell reached down to pet Pooch, saying, "Good boy. You've been doin' my job, haven't you? Taking care of my girl? Thank you, boy."

The dog licked James's fingers in appreciation.

"Dad," said Maeve, "I'm really worried about Halloween this year. The Samhain celebration is the time when the dead can cross the boundary to the living, and I'm worried about Grandpa coming to hurt me. He's not the man you used to know and love. He's evil and has been for years. The beast does his bidding, and I don't know how to destroy it."

"This is a lot to think about, Maeve. It's pretty hard to take in and believe. I think I'll have a talk with Nelda this week and listen to what she has to say. She's always been a straight shooter."

"She's been great to me, and she'll fill you in on everything I told you and more. By the way, Dad, what was your meeting about?"

"I was plannin' to tell you in a few weeks, Maeve, but I guess it can't hurt to tell you now, considerin' everything you shared with me. I'm gonna' sell Grandpa's house. It's not worth much, but the land is, and we need the money."

"But, Pa, there are so many things in the house that mean something to me! You can't be serious!" Maeve protested.

"You'd best get your friend to help you box up whatever you want to keep, Maeve. A bulldozer is coming at the end of the month to raze the house and clear the land. It's all settled."

Maeve was quiet for a few moments. It was true that the house and its contents had a special place in her heart, but her grandfather's new persona eroded much of her affection for it. She definitely wanted the old photos. Maeve believed she should return the Celtic book to Nelda, since it did, after all, belong to Goody originally.

"All right, Dad. I'll ring up Sylvie and ask her to help me save some things from the old house. We'll get some boxes from the supermarket and go over there next weekend. By the way, I'm supposed to sleep at Sylvie's next weekend. I hope that's still okay."

"No problem, Maeve. I'll stay here and spend the time goin' through old papers I found in my father's house a few days ago. I need to find the deed, among other important documents."

"Deal," said Maeve, and there was a definite spring in her step as she headed to the kitchen to prepare dinner for the two of them. Behind her, she heard the clinking of glass bottles as her father tossed his liquor bottles into the trash. She smiled at the unfamiliar sound. Next, she called Aunt Nelda.

"Hi, Aunt Nelda. Is there any room in your house to store Papa Will's possessions? My pa is having the house torn down, and there are things I think we should save," she explained.

"Of course, my dear. There's lots of room in my place. Box up what you want to save and come on over."

Maeve smiled. She called Sylvie and they arranged to go to the local supermarket, and then Papa Will's place, the following weekend. Maeve was excited by the prospect of spending more time with Sylvie going through Papa Will's possessions. There had to be some hidden treasures in the old house. As an extra bonus, she was going to have the opportunity to visit Nelda and have one of her amazing meals. What excited Maeve most was the chance to introduce Sylvie to Nelda. She'd been wanting to introduce them for months, and she couldn't wait for them to finally meet.

Chapter 26

The following weekend, Sylvie and Maeve ran to the supermarket to collect boxes. The manager was pleased to be rid of them, so the girls happily transported the empty containers to what they called "Papa Will's place." They dragged the boxes into the living room and looked around.

"It's weird, knowing that this house is going to be taken down to the ground," Maeve remarked.

"Yeah, but we'll take out anything that has special meaning for you before that happens, Maeve."

Maeve smiled. "Let's get started upstairs in the attic. We'll hunt down all the old photos we can find. Identifying these people will be a cool research project for us when we're done with the cold cases. I guess we're almost done with them since we understand now what happened to Elizabeth and my mom," she added with a note of sadness.

"Yeah, and I think we can guess what happened to the deputies," Sylvie concluded.

"Yes," replied Maeve. "I'll need to talk to the sheriff about that. Then he'll be able to close the books on my mom's murder and the deputies' critical conditions."

"And he'll also be able to identify what creature overturned our bus on the camping trip," Sylvie said.

"Yeah, I regret not telling him the complete truth, but I didn't want to panic the townspeople until I knew more about how the pieces fit together."

"I think you did the right thing," Sylvie commented. "Now let's get up to the attic and get busy. We don't want to be here too late, just in case...you know."

The girls sped up the stairs and got busy sorting the photos into boxes. It took them the better part of the afternoon. Maeve boxed *The Encyclopedia of Celtic Lore.* She wasn't sure what she would do with it, but she wasn't ready to let it go yet. Next, the girls explored Papa Will's bedroom. Sylvie moved the bookcase to find anything of value that might be on the wall.

"Look, Maeve! It's a hidden panel. I wonder if there is anything in it?"

Maeve rushed over to look, and the two girls pried the panel open with an old screwdriver they found in the attic. To their surprise, they discovered two mysterious boxes that Papa Will must have hidden there.

"Oh, my goodness," cried Maeve. "These boxes might hold the keys to all the horrible things that have happened in Wren Falls! The beast is still on the loose, so let's bring them with these other boxes to Nelda's while it's still light out. She'll have an idea what to do with them. She said she'd store Papa's stuff for me. This is probably the stuff that came from Goody."

"Who's Goody?"

"That's a story for another time."

"Fine. Let's go. I'm starving." Sylvie and Maeve skipped out the door, juggling two boxes each at the same time. They figured they'd get a pretty decent meal at Nelda's.

She never disappoints.

Maeve followed Sylvie out the door.

Sheriff Zen was completely frustrated. His search party was unable to find the predator that had been stalking Wren Falls and its inhabitants for the better part of a year. He'd visited Don several times at the hospital, and while the visits always began well, they quickly deteriorated as soon as he brought up the topic of Deputy Henry's assault. The visits always ended with Don screaming about some creature before he fell into a dead silence.

"I'm going to have one more go at Maeve," he murmured to himself. "I'm sure she knows more than she's told me." So, on his way home from one of these fruitless hospital visits, he made a quick detour to Maeve's house. *I'm going to get to the bottom of this once and for all. I'll bet the deputies' conditions are tied somehow to the school bus incident, and I'm going to find out the connection if it's the last thing I do.*

Arriving at Maeve's house about fifteen minutes later, the sheriff exited his police car and knocked on her door. There was no answer. He walked around to the back of the house and tried the rarely used back door, but again, no response. He returned to the front door and yelled, "Maeve, are you in there? It's Sheriff Zen. I need to talk to you. It's important!" From a distance, Zen heard what sounded like the cries of howling dogs. It startled him, but he kept his concentration on the task at hand. "Open up, Maeve, I'm sure you're in there! No hiding out in the laundry this time!" he yelled.

The sheriff glanced briefly to his right, shocked by what he spied out of the corner of his eye. Coming up the walkway was a creature with the large head of a snake, a lot like a king cobra, hooves like a deer, which he noticed striking the cement walkway, and the rest of the body being part leopard and part lion. He could detect the hissing of the snake's head and barely recovered his wits in time to race into his patrol car and slam the door shut, locking all of them. It very nearly *was* the last thing he ever did.

"Good grief," he muttered and began praying in earnest as the creature neared his car. A man of action, the sheriff called his dispatcher and radioed, "Sheriff down—needs assistance. *Immediately*! Calling for backup! Send multiple cars to Maeve Newell's house. Put on all sirens and come armed with heavy firepower, *now*! Do you read me, dispatcher?" he yelled into the radio.

"Yes, sir," came the response.

"All officers proceed with caution!" he added, and at that very moment, the creature began to slam into the squad car until it had successfully turned it over on its side. It began picking at the door handles with its venomous fangs, as the sheriff prayed that his men would arrive before it was too late.

The sound of police sirens pierced the air as six cars, three borrowed from a neighboring town, pulled up about twenty-five feet behind the sheriff's car. The men and women in the cars couldn't believe what they were looking at. None of them wanted to leave the safety of their vehicles to confront the beast in front of them.

"Get out of your cars, you damned cowards!" The sheriff yelled into the radio as he cowered in a corner of his vehicle hidden from view. "Unload your ammo on this thing! We're not taking it alive! This is what viciously attacked Deputy Henry and frightened Deputy Don half out of his wits. If you care about your fellow officers, get out of those cars and *fire*!"

The bravest of the lot climbed out first, shielding themselves behind the open car doors. They unloaded all their firepower on the beast, and the other officers joined them. Incredibly, the beast appeared unfazed by the weaponry and eventually, after a few spine-tingling growls, left the area unscathed. When it was out of sight, the police officers stopped their firing and helped right the sheriff's squad car. He emerged from the vehicle visibly shaken.

"Did you see that, officers? Our weapons didn't even make a dent in that creature. I don't know what it will take to kill it, but we have to find a way to finish it off. I've got a whole bunch of questions spinning around in my head. Good thing Maeve wasn't home today, after all. That thing is a threat to everyone in Wren Falls, and Halloween, which isn't far off, will be a great cover for this creature. We've got to kill it before it wreaks havoc on our town. Appreciate your assistance," he said, tilting his head in the direction of the neighboring policemen who volunteered for the dangerous assignment.

The sheriff gave the word, and they all piled into their respective cars, heading back to their station houses and relieved that they didn't have up close and personal contact with the creature.

"Gonna' be some crazy nightmares tonight," mumbled the sheriff as he climbed back into his car.

Sylvie and Maeve raced over to Papa Will's house. They were eager to rummage through it to find items that had special meaning for Maeve or just piqued their interest in general. The house was like an old treasure box that needed exploring before it was gone forever. Sylvie was also welcome to keep anything that was of interest to her. Many things were broken or in need of some simple repairs. Anything they chose to keep, they kept on the old sofa for the present. They had a more important mission: bringing the boxes that filled Papa's basement to Aunt Nelda's huge cellar. An old Radio Flyer wagon in Papa Will's basement provided a vehicle that could be used for that purpose.

"This must have been Dad's when he was a little boy," commented Maeve. "Let's load up these boxes in the wagon, and we can take turns pulling it."

Sylvie agreed, and the girls chattered endlessly as they transported the boxes to Aunt Nelda's. Mostly, Maeve filled Sylvie in on the amazing décor, furnishings, artifacts, and foods that she would experience at Nelda's house.

"You won't believe the place." Maeve grinned. "It's like a museum—the most fascinating museum you have ever seen. It's incredible!"

"I can't wait to see it, but tell me, what's Aunt Nelda like? I've never met her, but you're always talking about her."

"She's grand, Sylvie. She's so calm and reassuring, strong and courageous. She's also smart and generous. Aunt Nelda was my mom's best friend. She's not really my aunt, but she was like a sister to my mother, so I call her "Aunt". She welcomes you right away, as if she's known you for ages. She's positively magical!"

"Sounds like today will be one for the memory books," smiled Sylvie.

The girls finally reached Nelda's, and Sylvie admired the architecture of the building right away. It was unlike anything found in Wren Falls or nearby, for that matter. The house looked like a castle, with turrets and stained-glass windows.

"Gee, Maeve, all she's missing is the moat," Sylvie gawked.

"Yeah. She considered it but rejected it as a bit too ostentatious." Maeve laughed.

"Right," laughed Sylvie. "This place is so understated."

Maeve laughed and pulled the bell cord. Instantly, Nelda appeared in a golden caftan with a matching turban and elf-like slippers.

"Come in, come in, girls," she beckoned. "Who is this, Maeve?"

"Aunt Nelda, this is my friend, Sylvie," Maeve made the introductions.

"Ah, yes. Maeve has told me a lot about you, Sylvie. All good things to be sure." Nelda smiled.

"These are the things we saved from Papa Will's house. Pa sold it, and it will be razed to the ground." Maeve explained. "We want to store them in your home for a while if you don't mind. One of the boxes contains Goody's *The Codex Demonicus.* I believe you should have that."

"Of course, my child. There's plenty of storage space in my home for your possessions. I am especially grateful for the book," said Nelda. "Let me get these boxes out of the way and into the basement." And with a flick of her wrist, the boxes disappeared.

"How did she do that, Maeve?"

"She has her ways." Maeve winked in Nelda's direction.

They all continued into the living room, where Sylvie's eyes popped open as she scanned the exotic and elaborate furnishings and artifacts.

"What a room, Aunt Nelda," she exclaimed. "It's amazing!"

"Thank you, Sylvie. I'm glad you approve." Nelda grinned at Maeve. She explained the history of her décor and her artifacts for the next forty minutes or so.

"Are you hungry, girls? Have you had lunch?"

"No," said Maeve and Sylvie in unison. They laughed at the effect. "We came right over after we collected the boxes."

"Well then," said Nelda, "you must come into the dining room and have a bite to eat. I insist."

Walking into the next room, Sylvie couldn't believe the table set before them. Magnificent English bone China, Waterford crystal from Ireland, and flowered cloth napkins adorned the table. English tea sandwiches of all varieties, accompanied by an incredible array of fruits, both common and exotic, called to them. The three sat down and began to sample *everything*.

They washed down their meal with Earl Grey tea and pushed away from the table, full to bursting.

"I hope you left room for dessert, girls," mentioned Nelda.

The girls looked at each other, aghast.

"I suppose I could make some room for dessert," Maeve stated.

"I shall certainly try," agreed Sylvie.

"Excellent!" Nelda clapped her hands three times. An astounding array of pastries, including petits fours, marzipan, Danish, and sundry cookies, appeared on platters in the center of the table. They all ate their desserts with unbridled enthusiasm.

When it was time to leave, Maeve said, "It's getting late, and it will be dark soon. I think we'd better get going."

"Thanks so much, Aunt Nelda," said both girls.

"You're quite welcome. Don't worry about the cleanup, girls. I'll take care of it," said Nelda as she ushered the girls to the front door. Then she flicked her wrist in a backhanded motion, and the dishes completely disappeared. The table looked like it had never even been used.

Sylvie and Maeve, who had glanced back over their shoulders to take a last look at Nelda, caught her in the act. Sylvie whispered to Maeve, "How did she do *that*?"

Maeve just giggled. "Magic!"

It was too late for the girls to return to Will's place to retrieve the items on the old sofa that they had selected for themselves. That would have to be done at a later date. The risk of running into the Questing Beast increased as the sun lowered in the sky. They decided discretion was the better part of valor and agreed to get their souvenirs before the house was razed.

Chapter 27

Maeve's mind often went to thoughts of Sheriff Zen. She was not a person who typically told untruths, and it bothered her that she did not tell the sheriff the whole truth about the beast. She acknowledged that she would not be relieved of this guilt until she met with the sheriff and unburdened herself. Maeve told herself that the sheriff was not an unreasonable man, that he would understand her position, and that she would be better off being honest with him. She decided to go down to the police station and have a private conversation with him.

On a clear October day, two weeks after the visit to Nelda's house, Maeve strode down to the sheriff's office. It was only about a mile away if she took the shortcut through the woods. Lately, that had not been a viable option with the beast running rampant throughout the forest, so she took the long way around. She grabbed a bottle of water and began the three-mile hike to the center of Wren Falls. She was feeling better already, eager to get her confession off her chest. She imagined the sheriff being grateful for the information. She couldn't wait to update him on the strange goings-on in and around Wren Falls. *He'll finally understand what happened in the bus incident at the campgrounds last summer,* she said to herself with some satisfaction. *He'll be able to protect the town this Halloween because, as they say, "Knowledge is power."* She smiled at these thoughts and was feeling pretty good about herself.

Maeve took a swig of her water. It was unseasonably warm for October. She tried to walk on the shady side of the street under the large oaks, to cool off when she could. "Just another mile or so to go," she said aloud, thinking how great it would be to sit in the sheriff's air-conditioned office for a while, telling her story. "Sylvie would be proud of me."

When she was about a half mile from the station house, she began to be aware of the familiar cries of the beast. It was coming from the nearby woods, and Maeve hastened her step. A feeling of panic overtook her, and her adrenaline kicked in. Maeve raced to the sheriff's office and arrived, sweating profusely. She rapped loudly on his door, and she could hear him inside. He was pushing back his chair, scraping the floor, before he strolled leisurely to the entrance of the station house.

"Open up, Sheriff! Hurry!" Maeve called out. She noticed the beast from a distance, staring at her as it circled the outskirts of the town. The next minute seemed like thirty to Maeve. The sheriff stood in the doorway and beckoned her inside. Maeve pushed past him and slammed the door shut. "Lock it," she demanded.

"Where's the fire, Maeve?" Sheriff Zen asked in a slightly impatient tone, as he locked the door. He didn't like being ordered around by his townspeople, no less by a young girl.

"You'll understand after I tell you my story, Sheriff," Maeve answered. "I've wanted to give you some vital information for some time now, but I couldn't. I didn't want to panic the townspeople. Also, I was sure you'd believe I was crazy and would never accept my account."

"Does this have anything to do with the bus incident, Maeve?" Sheriff Zen inquired.

"That and more," she shook her head in the affirmative as she spoke.

"I'm listening." He leaned forward in his favorite chair and offered Maeve a cold Coke, which she took gladly. After gulping down half the bottle, Maeve began to speak. She went all the way back to Elizabeth Hathaway's macabre demise, and the sheriff listened in disbelief. She told him of her research with Sylvie, but left Nelda out of the telling. Maeve didn't want her interrogated by the police and decided to leave her out of the account.

Maeve went into the details of her mother's brutal murder, and she described for the sheriff the uncanny commonalities between the two crimes. Then came a very difficult admission—Maeve had to confess her grandfather's part in both crimes.

The sheriff shook his head as he listened to Maeve's retelling of the events. "Impossible. I was well-acquainted with the man. He wouldn't have been capable of committing such evil acts."

Maeve described the transformation of her grandfather when he believed Elizabeth had betrayed him. "Betrayal was the impetus for his changeover to an evildoer," explained Maeve. "He became involved with a creature found in the Celtic myths, the Questing Beast. The two became connected, and Papa Will's wish was the beast's command. Ever since Papa Will's death, the beast has run rampant throughout our region, specifically around Wren Falls."

"Are you telling me that a mythological creature has been responsible for several deaths in this area, and you've known this for some time, Maeve?"

"Yes, sir," she added.

"If I had knowledge of all of this before, Maeve, I might have been able to prevent Deputy Henry's savage attack and Deputy Don's psychotic break," his voice rose. "Deputy Henry has a wife and two children. These two deputies are the best I have, and they are fine men! Not to mention," he said, "the events at the summer camp, where several students and Miss Clouder were seriously injured. Did you know about this beast then?"

"Yes, sir," answered Maeve with a sheepish look on her face.

"Then, why in hell didn't you tell me this? I would never have sent just two deputies out into the forest to conduct a search had I known what they would be facing. Oh, my God!" he yelled. "Annabeth Morgan was right all along!"

"Yes, sir. She was," confessed Maeve. The interview was not going the way she had anticipated. She was feeling very guilty, and tears were beginning to form behind her eyes.

"Why in the world did you keep this a damned secret, Maeve?" Zen stomped around his tiny office.

"I told you, sir. You'd think I was crazy and wouldn't believe me. I didn't want to cause a panic in town and hoped the beast would eventually disappear. But now with Halloween coming, I'm afraid it will take advantage of Samhain's traditions to wreak havoc on the town and its residents. I'm telling you all this so you can be prepared. You will need many extra officers to deal with the situation. I can draw you a picture of what the beast looks like. That should help."

"Thanks for the heads up, Maeve," Sheriff Zen said with biting sarcasm. "But I've already had a personal introduction outside your house."

"My house? When?" asked Maeve.

"A few days ago, when I came to speak with you again. You weren't home."

"Oh, my gosh!,"

"Oh, my gosh, is right, Maeve. That creature nearly destroyed my squad car, and none of the firepower that my patrolmen and women used was effective against it. We were lucky no one was killed," he added. "I have no idea how to destroy this creature, do you?"

"No, Sheriff Zen. I have no idea how it can be destroyed, but we need to come up with something before Samhain arrives."

The sheriff looked at Maeve with a mixture of rage and disgust on his face. "I should arrest you right now and throw away the key," he said loudly. Sheriff Zen was in a real pickle because of her, and he recognized that. He left her sitting in his office and stormed out the door.

Maeve lay awake in her bed that night, thinking about the sheriff's words. She replayed them in her head over and over again. Maeve hadn't ever connected the events of the summer and the fate of the deputies to her own inaction. She hadn't realized that these incidents could have been prevented if she'd gone to the sheriff originally. She was directly responsible for the terrible things that befell others in the town, as well. The guilt was overpowering, and Maeve began to cry until her body was wracked with sobs. She wished there was a way to undo the evil happenings, but she could not think of a solution. Not until Pooch climbed into her bed and curled up next to her did she begin to relax and eventually fall into a troubled sleep.

This time, her dream was about the beast itself. It chased her through the oaks, making frightening sounds that sent chills up her spine. The fierce cries of the creature, mixed with the hissing sounds from the snake head. The pounding of the hooves told her that it was coming closer every second. Maeve ran to Nelda's, but the door was bolted. She kept banging on the door to no avail. Maeve's calls for help went unheard, and finally the creature's fangs caught up with her and sank into her neck. There was no time left to be saved.

Maeve woke up with a start. She rubbed her neck and checked for blood. She shivered, and her body ached all over. Maeve couldn't catch her breath. Pooch was nowhere to be found, and her fear was palpable.

"Pooch, Pooch, where are you?"

There was no response.

Outside her window, a familiar cackling sound—her grandfather's laugh!—confronted her. Turning to her right, looking out her casement window, the familiar snake head was staring at her with its red eyes boring into her brain, while its forked tongue taunted her. Eventually, Pooch returned to her room, and when Maeve looked out the windows, the snake head was gone, and Papa Will's laugh was silenced.

The weekend of her sleepover at Sylvie's house was near. Maeve had so much to reveal to her friend. She especially wanted to tell her all about the conversation with Sheriff Zen. She needed to share it with Sylvie and get her thoughts on the matter. Maeve was still reeling from the experience, but she tried to put it out of her head and think only of the weekend to come. She packed a small travel bag for her overnight at Sylvie's and brought it to school with her.

Maeve also wanted to share her dream with Sylvie. It was one of the most horrifying she'd experienced, and she needed to get it out of her conscious mind. Besides Aunt Nelda, Sylvie was the only one she was comfortable sharing it with. Things had improved a lot with Maeve's dad, but he was still adjusting to the news he had received about the deaths in his family, and Maeve didn't think he needed more to contend with.

The school day seemed to last forever. The girls had exciting plans for the weekend. Next week was Halloween, and they were going to spend time decorating Sylvie's house and preparing items that could be placed outside as well, to help create the holiday atmosphere. Sylvie's father brought home an assortment of pumpkins in different sizes for the girls to carve. They were going to bake special Halloween treats and create a tasty orange punch with gummy worms floating on the surface. There were other activities planned, as well. Maeve couldn't wait for the weekend to begin. Pooch was staying home with Pa for the weekend.

When the school day finally ended, Sylvie and Maeve collected their backpacks and Maeve's overnight bag and headed for Sylvie's house. They chatted about their plans for the weekend and were in high spirits until they detected hoof beats in the distance.

"We'd better get a move on," whispered Maeve.

"Yeah, we don't want to run into any unwelcome company."

The hoof beats grew louder.

"Run!" said Maeve.

They took off like a shot. The girls rounded the corner to Sylvie's front door just in time to run inside and bolt it. The beast hurled its body against the side of the house.

"What in tarnation is that noise?" called Sylvie's dad, who was preparing things in the kitchen. The girls stared at him wide-eyed, unable to answer. He moved to the front window in the living room and pulled aside the curtain. His face turned grey and then white. His lips were blue. When he started to get his wits about him, Mr. Hoffmann ran for his hunting rifle and flew upstairs to the second landing. He opened the bedroom window about halfway and fired at the beast's head. He emptied his gun and reloaded when the creature turned around and disappeared into the adjacent woods.

Sylvie ran upstairs to check on her father and found him pale and slumped on the floor against the hallway wall.

"Dad! Dad! Are you okay?" she asked him.

"I'll be all right, Sylvie. Can you get me some water? I need to catch my breath."

Sylvie hurried to get a glass of water for her dad, while Maeve just stared at him, open-mouthed. Then she looked at the empty hunting rifle lying next to Mr. Hoffmann.

A few minutes after Sylvie returned with the water, her father asked, "What *was* that thing, girls?" He turned towards his daughter and repeated his question. "What *was* that creature, girls?" It looked just like the picture I found in your room that day, Sylvie. You said it was for a contest. I think you have some explaining to do."

Sylvie went into her bedroom and rummaged around in her closet. She emerged from her room, holding a painting wrapped in newspaper.

"Unwrap that, please," said her father.

She slowly let the newspaper fall to the floor so the painting was in full view. Maeve gasped. She couldn't believe the likeness between the painting and the actual creature.

"My God, Sylvie. You are really talented! It actually gives me the creeps!" she said.

"What is this thing, Sylvie?" asked her dad.

Sylvie and Maeve told Mr. Hoffmann about the beast. They didn't get into Maeve's grandfather, and Maeve didn't bring up Nelda. They limited their information to the fact that it was a mythological Celtic creature capable of inflicting terror and violence and was especially active around Halloween. That was enough. Mr. Hoffmann was becoming agitated.

"That's it, Sylvie," her dad stated firmly. "No trick-or-treating for you this Halloween. I want you home where you are safe. You stay inside until the holiday is over. I'm also going to have a talk with the sheriff. I want to know exactly what he is doing about this problem and how he plans to keep the town safe on Halloween." He strode out of the room, and the girls were left alone, finally.

Sylvie looked crushed.

"Maybe it's a good thing that he found out," Maeve offered. "You won't have to keep secrets from him, and maybe he can help."

"How?" asked Sylvie.

"I don't know. We'll just have to wait and see. Maybe he'll let you come to *my* house on Halloween. We don't have to go out. We can have fun together inside."

"I guess so," said Sylvie. "I wonder what will come of his discussion with the sheriff."

"Speaking of the sheriff, Sylvie, I have to tell you about *my* conversation with him. I went down to the station house to tell him the truth about the bus incident at the camping grounds and to warn him about the beast."

"Maeve, no! You didn't want him to know about the beast—you were afraid to panic the townspeople!"

"I used to believe that, Sylvie. I also didn't think he'd believe me, and he would think I was a nutcase. He was furious with me! He said if I'd told him the truth earlier, then a lot of people would have been spared serious injuries, like our teacher and Deputy Henry. He blamed me for Deputy Don's breakdown and told me I should be arrested!"

"Oh, no, Maeve! How awful!"

"To top it off, he already *was aware of* the beast! He'd had a bad run-in with it at my house just a few days ago! So, I guess keeping secrets from the sheriff and your father has only added to the crisis in our town. Now your father is going to talk with the sheriff, and he'll learn how rotten a person I am."

"I don't know what to say, Maeve. Did you tell the sheriff all about your grandpa and your mom's murder?"

"I told him just about everything, but I left out Nelda. There's no reason to drag her into this mess," said Maeve.

The two girls sat quietly for a few minutes, each deep in thought.

"Come on, let's not let this ruin our weekend. We can start making our Halloween treats in the kitchen and carving our pumpkins," suggested Sylvie.

"I'm game," said Maeve. "Let's forget about the beast for one night."

"Yeah, but will the beast forget about us tonight?" asked Sylvie.

Chapter 28

The superstitious residents of Wren Falls take their Celtic myths and legends very seriously. As Halloween approached, people mumbled about Samhain and grumbled about the strange goings-on in the past year. References to the weird bus accident when the school children were returning from their camping experience, the bizarre description of the predator given by Annabeth Morgan, the strange attack on Deputy Henry, and other peculiar sightings and sounds observed by some of the populace gave fodder to otherworldly speculation. No rational explanation for these events had evolved, and citizens were noticeably skittish about the upcoming holiday. Sylvie's dad, Mr. Hoffmann, joined the police officers and other volunteers in patrolling the area and safeguarding the residents.

The night of October 31st was when the boundary between the dead and the living became permeable. The dead could come through that curtain of time and roam amongst the living. The requisite bonfire was still scheduled, and folks were still planning to dress in costumes to scare away the ghosts and goblins. The people of Wren Falls decorated the town with traditional Halloween displays and carved jack-o-lanterns with large candles that would be ablaze during the evening. All of this was done with some hesitancy—a look-over-your–shoulder attitude infused the adults since the arrival of the monster stalking the town. The children were young enough and naïve enough to embrace the holiday with enthusiasm.

Maeve was uneasy. She had a nagging feeling that something big was about to happen tonight. She'd had enough warnings from Aunt Nelda not to take anything for granted. Her dreams about Papa Will had grown steadily more frightening. She would be alone for a good part of the night until Sylvie and Nelda joined her for some Halloween refreshments and storytelling. Pa would be helping with the activities this year around the bonfire. She didn't expect him to get home in time to celebrate with her and her guests. She told herself to calm down and focus on decorating the living room, where she expected to host Sylvie and Nelda. Pooch was staying at Nelda's for the night. A movement to her left caused Maeve to look at her window, and a large black bird was staring at her. Her mind went to Morrigan, foreteller of doom, who often shapeshifted into the form of a black bird before someone died. She shuddered.

Forcing herself to focus on creating the right ambience, Maeve lit an assortment of candles and placed them in a variety of locations around the living room. They represented all colors, shapes, and sizes, and when she finished, she admired her handiwork as playful shadows danced on the walls. Maeve, in her sleek black cat costume, played with her own shadow, making movements like a cat, stretching and pawing the air. *I wonder how Sylvie and Nelda will be dressed?* As she moved around the room enjoying the eerie atmosphere, the worry came back to her, suffocating her, wrapping itself around her torso like a tight-fitting glove. It was Samhain, and she was aware, too, that Papa Will was at his most evil during that time.

"I'm being silly," she said aloud and went back to her decorating. Her favorite piece of décor was a large pumpkin that she had carved herself. It had a large, lit candle centered in its base and a scowling, toothless grin on its visage. She surrounded the pumpkin with plastic bones to complete the effect. Maeve glanced at the old mantle clock that her mother treasured and noticed that it was almost eight p.m. *I can't wait for Nelda and Sylvie to arrive. It's spooky being here on Halloween all by myself, and it's already really dark outside.*

"It will be too late by then, my dear," said a deep, unfamiliar voice.

Maeve spun around and found herself face to face with her grandfather's spirit.

"What are you doing here?" she asked him, taking in the long black cloak and fedora, noting his skeletal face and hands. A red glow surrounded him. *He has no shadow,* she realized, trembling. Her fingers closed around a snow globe with an evil eye inside it. She had purchased it at the local party store. Maeve hid it behind her back.

"Is that any way to greet your Papa Will, Maeve?" he asked, cackling for a few seconds. He seemed to be enjoying her fear. "You realize it's Samhain. I do my best work on Samhain. You must have been expecting me."

"What do you want?" asked Maeve.

"I should think that would be obvious, dear child. I have come to destroy you."

Maeve hurled the globe at her grandfather. He caught it with his bony fingers, and it disintegrated. He smirked. She backed further away from him in a state of panic.

Stalling for time, Maeve tried to think of a way to defend herself. She moved closer to the pumpkin as she asked, "Why do you want to hurt me? You loved me, Papa Will." He pushed forward in Maeve's direction.

"That was another time, Maeve. Things have changed. You went against my wishes and kept up your investigations. You told my son that he was *not* my son and that I was behind Alice's murder. He hates me now, and I cannot forgive you for betraying me."

His eyes flashed, and Maeve recalled Nelda's comment that betrayal was what sent Papa Will on his spiral descent into Evil, going back to Elizabeth's murder. Drool dripped from his rotted mouth, and for the first time, she noted the yellowish cast of his hollowed-out eye sockets. She trembled, and her fear was palpable. She was very close to the pumpkin now.

"On top of all that," his voice got louder, "You have uncovered my ties to the Questing Beast and ruined my reputation in Wren Falls. I can't let you live!" Papa Will lunged for Maeve's throat, his skeletal fingers tightening around it.

Just as the last words came out of his mouth, Pa entered the house. Perceiving the danger to his daughter, he yelled, "Get away from her!" and tried to grab Papa Will's arms. Will just laughed and continued to squeeze Maeve's throat with his putrid fingers. James Newell lunged at his father and tried to pull him away from Maeve, but Papa Will threw him against the wall with uncharacteristic strength, and Maeve's dad slumped to the floor, injured. He was losing consciousness.

At the same time, Maeve grabbed the lit jack-o-lantern and threw it at her grandfather's cloak. It ignited immediately. Papa Will let out a blood-curdling scream, and as he burned, the door flew open. The Questing Beast raced into the room, pawing the air and roaring ferociously. The beast was in position to pounce on Maeve, but just when she expected to be another Samhain victim, her grandfather disintegrated into a pile of smoking ashes. The beast let out a cry of pain and approached Papa Will's remains. It groaned, slowly rolled over onto its side, and died.

From the ashes, Maeve detected her grandpa's natural voice saying, "Thank you, Maeve." She glanced at the nearest wall and discovered a new shadow on it—that of the smoldering ashes.

In the next few moments, the beast disappeared, and Nelda appeared at the door with Sylvie, who was dressed as an alluring vampire. Nelda was dressed as, what else? A witch. She was, after all, a real witch, and her everyday outfits were her costumes. Maeve smiled as she realized she was probably the only person in town who recognized this. She rubbed her sore neck and crawled over to her father.

"We got here just in time for your grandpa's last words and to witness the beast's demise," Nelda informed Maeve.

"What happened to the beast?".

"It was finally destroyed, Maeve. Its connection to your grandfather was so strong. it could not live if your grandpa's spirit died. You have saved the people of Wren Falls. I just took out the garbage with my handy red dust." Nelda smiled.

Maeve was on the floor, talking softly to her father. "You were very brave, Dad. You tried to save me, and I'll never forget that. Right now, we need to get you to the doctor to be examined." They would have to take him to a nearby medical center in the next town. Her father nodded in agreement.

"Are you all right, Maeve?" asked Sylvie, concerned.

"I'm okay, Sylvie, but I have lots of questions."

"Tomorrow is soon enough for questions, Maeve. Let's get you and your father some help and get away from here," said Nelda.

"Good idea, Aunt Nelda," answered Maeve, and the three of them helped James Newell to his feet and slowly walked out the door. At the same time, Maeve handed Nelda her *Encyclopedia of Celtic Lore.*

"I think I've had enough of the Celtic stories to last me a while," Maeve glanced. at Nelda. Just at that moment, there was a great chorus of cawing birds, and Sylvie pointed to the sky. "Look, it's a flock of ravens!"

"It's Morrigan's flock," explained Nelda. "They are leaving Wren Falls, and that, my dears, is a very good sign." She turned to Maeve and winked at her. It was a signal meant for Maeve only, and she received it gratefully.

The rest of the holiday passed uneventfully. People wore costumes, attended bonfires, and celebrated Samhain in all the traditional ways. They were unaware of what had transpired in Maeve's house and that true Evil died there. James Newell went to Nelda's house after a brief evaluation in the medical center, where a local doctor attended to his wounds. The girls called the sheriff. He learned about the events of the evening from Maeve and Sylvie and breathed a heavy sigh of relief.

"Whew! Thank God that beast is gone, and we can get back to a bit of normalcy in Wren Falls," he remarked. "No one here is to tell the residents about the beast or its connection to Will Newell. My men have all been instructed to keep this information a secret so as not to panic the citizens."

"But, Sheriff, isn't keeping secrets what caused all the trouble in the first place?" asked Maeve. She exchanged a knowing look with Sylvie.

"It's been a long night, young lady. I will not be interrogated by a teenaged girl. Take your father home and get some rest. We'll close the chapter on these events tonight and never speak of them again." The sheriff turned and left immediately, relieved to get back to his normal patrolling.

"Wow," exclaimed Sylvie. "That was unexpected."

"Yeah," Maeve agreed. "I've had enough secrets to last me a lifetime. I think I'll disregard that advice." The two girls walked outside into the crisp Halloween air.

"It's great to be able to walk without fear again," Maeve confided to Sylvie as they strolled through the town's streets, enjoying their Halloween treats.

Chapter 29

About two weeks later, when James had healed from his injuries, Maeve asked to have some time to discuss a few things with him. He agreed, and they proceeded to the small living room. She was nervous about how he would respond to what she was about to divulge.

"I need to talk to you about Aunt Nelda, Pa."

"What about her? I know you two have become quite close, and she was very helpful on Halloween night," he commented.

"Yeah, we are close," said Maeve. "What I tell you is just between us, okay, Dad? I've learned that keeping secrets can be dangerous, but in this case, *not* keeping one could be dangerous to someone I care for deeply—Nelda."

"I'm not following, Maeve. What do you mean?"

"Dad, when Papa Will came to this country from Ireland, he settled in Salem, Massachusetts, for a while."

"Right, go on," Pa encouraged her.

"At that time, he became very friendly with a woman named Goody Webster. She was actually a Light Witch, which means that she helped people with their problems, using charms, potions, and incantations—in other words, she used good magic. She and Papa Will were very close. He boarded in her house and told no one about her special abilities."

"This is all news to me," Pa commented.

"Unfortunately, an anti-witch fever swept Salem at that time, and witches were being rounded up and punished for practicing Dark Magic, even if they were really innocent. The town elders killed many of them. Goody was one of those unfortunate people who was tried and judged guilty. She was hanged after her sentencing."

"Good Lord!" uttered Maeve's father.

"Yes, Dad. It was an awful time. Before Goody was hanged, she gave Papa Will a secret book that he was to keep safe and away from prying eyes. No one was to know of its existence. He didn't want the responsibility, but there was no one else she trusted, so he agreed to hide the book and keep the secret," Maeve explained. "In return, Goody granted him longevity, but not immortality. The price he would pay for living several lifetimes was infertility. He would not be able to produce his own children. It would be too dangerous for them, living in the house with the book's evildoers."

"Maeve, I'm confused. He did produce a child. Me," said Maeve's father.

"I'm getting to that, Dad. It will all become clear to you in a minute," she answered.

"What was in this book, Maeve?" asked her father.

"It was called *The Codex Demonicus,* and it contained all the evils on earth. It was Papa Will's job to make sure they didn't escape and cause death and destruction throughout the world," answered Maeve. "Papa Will relocated and kept her book safe."

"He was a good and decent man until he was betrayed by his wife, your mother, Elizabeth. She had an affair with a neighbor that resulted in your birth. Papa Will confronted Elizabeth, and she admitted that the child was not his. That betrayal plunged Papa Will into a world of Evil. He begged Goody to help him get revenge for the betrayal and reminded her of the favor he had done for her by guarding her book all these years. With Goody's reluctant assistance, Papa Will planned his revenge on Elizabeth, which led to her untimely death. Because of that, Goody was sent to the Netherworld and was forbidden to have anything to do with humans for a century. Papa Will used the book to conjure up a monster, the Questing Beast. That vicious predator destroyed Elizabeth in a horrifying way. When he thought Alice, your wife and my mother, was involved with a neighbor as well, the prospect of another betrayal set him off again. He planned her death, too. Papa Will used the same incantation to call the beast and had Alice murdered, even though she was really innocent." James Newell sat there with his head in his hands.

"Oh, Maeve, you're describin' a man I didn't know. He wasn't the father I grew up with," said James sadly.

"I know, Pa. He wasn't the grandpa I loved, either," Maeve said. "He was willing to destroy his own granddaughter, assuming I had betrayed him It is just too much to wrap my brain around. But the secret I'm going to reveal is about Nelda."

"There's more? What about her?" her father asked.

"You may have noticed, Pa, that she has some unusual abilities. That is because she is the reincarnation of Goody Webster, the Light Witch. Goody equals Nelda!"

"What?" asked Pa, astonished. "You go too far, girl. You expect me to believe that? First, the news about my dad, I mean the man whom I considered to be my dad, and now you tell me that your mother's closest friend is a witch?"

"Yes, Pa. If you think back to some of the things that have happened and Nelda's part in them, you'll realize I'm right. Besides, I've actually seen her change from Nelda into Goody right before my eyes! This can't get out, because she won't be safe if her other identity is revealed."

"I think I'm getting a migraine." Pa turned towards his old liquor cabinet. "I could use a shot of my old whiskey."

"Those days are gone, Pa. You promised never to drink again. What you need to do is focus on a trade that you would like to do, so that we can afford to stay in Wren Falls. Then I won't have to worry where our next meal is coming from," admonished Maeve.

"I know, Maeve. I know. I'll keep my word, but you must promise me, no more secrets between us. You've given me a lot to get used to already today."

"Sounds like a plan, Dad. Now let's get to work deciding how we're going to use Grandpa's land. Seems to me we should repurpose it for something good. This town could use a facelift," she added.

"We'll puzzle that out after lunch, Maeve," he offered. "I'm starved!"

James put his arm around his daughter for the first time since his wife's death. Maeve enjoyed the warmth of his embrace. It was really good to be close to him, the way she used to be before Alice's demise. The two of them walked out into the sunshine, and the warmth of the sun mirrored the warmth in her heart. They walked to the Little Piggy lunch spot that Maeve had so often gone to with Sylvie and enjoyed their first meal together in almost a year. Maeve looked up at her father as she ate her burger and noticed him smiling. She returned the smile and said, "Welcome back, Pa."

A few hours later, Sylvie called Maeve. "Hey, how about we visit Nelda and share the contents of Papa Will's boxes with her? She said she'd like to see what was in them."

"Great idea, Sylvie," Maeve replied. "We packed everything up in a hurry, and there are some things I'd like a closer look at. Besides, there was one box that was already packed up when I got there. I guess my grandpa packed it himself so no one would see what was in it." Maeve called Aunt Nelda to ask if she could search the boxes from Papa Will's house. She mentioned that Sylvie was also interested in coming.

"Wonderful," replied Nelda. "I've been dying to explore them myself!" A visit was planned for that afternoon. The girls hurried to Aunt Nelda's house, and just as they started to pull the cord for the chimes, the door magically opened.

"How does she do that stuff?" queried Sylvie.

"What can I say? Nelda has her *own* secrets, Sylvie."

Sylvie rolled her eyes and noticed Nelda standing in the doorway.

"Welcome, girls. Why are you just standing out there? Come in, come in!" The three of them embraced, and Maeve asked, "Where are Papa's boxes, Aunt Nelda?"

"Just down there," she pointed to a closed black door, which instantly opened on its own, revealing a rickety staircase leading into a gloomy basement, dark as pitch. The girls looked askance at the sight.

"Is there a light?" asked Sylvie.

"No, my dear," answered Aunt Nelda. This house is over four hundred years old. People in those days used tapers. I like to keep the old traditions." With that, she pulled a long, lit candle from her caftan. The girls gasped. "Come on, girls, let's go! I'll lead," she offered, seeing their reluctance.

They gingerly made their way downstairs, holding onto the wooden banister that had seen better days. It was wobbly and unstable. Maeve decided she was safer *not* holding onto it and walked down the stairs sideways and slowly instead. When they reached the bottom, Nelda swiftly pulled another dozen lit tapers from her caftan and placed them around the room, leaving an eerie glow on the cracked walls.

"Hmm," murmured Nelda. "I've got to get this foundation repaired one of these centuries."

The three women walked over to a corner of the room and began to search through the boxes.

They discovered the nameless photos and asked Nelda if she could identify any of the subjects.

She stared at the photos for a second and said, "Oh yes, Maeve. These are some of your many relatives, long gone. I remember them well. We will have to sit down one day and identify them for posterity."

Sylvie and Maeve spent the whole afternoon rifling through the Newell artifacts, with Aunt Nelda's help. Finally, adorned with dust and spider webs, there were only two boxes left.

They were creepy-looking black boxes that matched the ambience of the musty room. Each had "*Danger!*" written on all sides and one prominent drawing of a skull and crossbones on the top.

"We didn't pack these," Sylvie noted.

"No, we sure didn't. They were hidden behind a secret panel in Papa Will's bedroom," Maeve confirmed.

"Girls, we need to open them very carefully," warned Nelda. "These boxes could be connected to the evil doings of your grandfather, Maeve."

As Maeve began picking at the binding on the first box, a purple cloud erupted from inside. After a substantial coughing spell, she was able to open the flaps and look inside.

Nelda pulled out a black robe and several dozen long black tapers. "These must be what your grandpa used when he was casting his evil spells," she speculated.

Sylvie found some test tubes labeled Mouse Tongue, Black Nightshade, Nighty Night—a sleeping draught, and several other unseemly specimens. "These must have been useful when he was practicing his Dark Arts," she whispered.

In the second box, Maeve found some dusty old tomes. Blowing off the dust, she noticed one called *The Codex Demonicus.* There was a black string used as a placeholder in the middle of the book. Maeve opened the book where the string marked a particular page. She began reading aloud: "*Nomine Demonicus voyis ayudan...*"

"Stop that this instant!" shouted Nelda. She snatched the book away from Maeve, slammed it shut, and buried it at the bottom of the box. "That is the spell your grandfather used to destroy the people he wanted to punish! You almost started the whole evil cycle again!"

Maeve burst out crying as Sylvie shuddered and moved away from the box. "I'm so sorry, Aunt Nelda. I didn't realize what I was doing."

Nelda put her arms around Maeve until she was able to stop sobbing.

"There, there. I forgive you, Maeve." Nelda gave Maeve one of her special Parisian handkerchiefs to wipe away her tears.

"I think this is a good time to bury this box under the others and to get out of this basement," as she hugged Maeve.

The girls agreed. They put out the tapers, folded up the robe with the books wrapped in it, stuffed the test tubes in the corners of the box, and shoved the box in the corner of the room, with the remaining boxes on top of it. They didn't breathe clean air until they climbed the staircase and exited the room, sighing with relief and coughing from the dust.

Chapter 30

On October 31st, at the stroke of midnight, the curtain between the dead and the living closed. November 1st was a day of miracles. No sooner had the dawn arrived than Deputy Henry began to heal. Starting with his feet, the blood began flowing to his legs, torso, chest, back, and arms, spreading to his head, rejuvenating his brain. His pulse began to stabilize, his breathing became more regular, and his fingers and toes began to move. In the next twenty-four hours, Deputy Henry was able to press the buzzer next to his bed to ask a floor nurse for a glass of water. He was able to see clearly, and with assistance, he could raise himself into a sitting position.

Henry was, at first, confused. *Where am I?* he wondered to himself. "How did I get here?" he asked the nurse who was attending him.

She was astounded by his progress. For months, he had been almost a vegetable, hooked up to various apparatus to keep him alive. Now, the nurse disconnected all of these tubes and machines, and it looked like he would be going home shortly.

"You are a very lucky man," commented the nurse. "When you came in here, I didn't think you'd last the night. Now, you're almost well enough to go home. It's a miracle!" she concluded.

In a separate wing of the hospital, Deputy Don was also showing remarkable progress. He seemed relaxed and had no psychotic episodes today. He appeared lucid and rational. He was properly oriented and spoke of the frightening encounter in the forest without any extreme reaction. It looked as if he, too, would be leaving the hospital in a short while. His nurse called Sheriff Zen to give him the good news about Don's improvement. Deputy Henry's nurse had already informed the sheriff of *his* progress, and Zen could barely contain his excitement.

He said to his wife, "My boys are coming home, hon! Can you believe it? They're both doing well and will be home in a few days! I have to tell the rest of the squad—we need to prepare a real homecoming for them. It's a miracle!"

The sheriff literally danced joyfully around his living room, holding his wife in his arms. She couldn't remember when she had last seen him so happy, but it was a welcome change from the past year. The sheriff excused himself, explaining to his wife that he had an important errand to run. He got into his squad car and headed for Maeve's house.

Sheriff Zen rapped on Maeve's front door. James answered and was surprised to see the sheriff standing there.

"Yes, Sheriff Zen? Can I help you?" he asked.

"Actually, I came to speak to Maeve."

"Is anything wrong, Sheriff?" asked James, a worried look on his face.

"No, no, I just came to give her some good news." Zen smiled.

"Okay, I'll get her." James expelled a sigh of relief. "Maeve! Sheriff Zen's here for you. Come in, Sheriff."

Maeve came into the room hesitantly. Her last encounter with the sheriff had been less than pleasant. "Yes, Sheriff?"

"Sit down, Maeve."

Maeve took a seat and looked at the sheriff inquisitively. He began. "We are all aware that October 31st, Halloween, is during the Samhain festival in the Celtic culture. It's a time when the dead can cross over to the world of the living." He looked at Maeve, who nodded in the affirmative.

"You also are also aware that both deputies, Henry and Don, were in critical condition in the hospital in the next town. Henry in very poor physical condition, Don in a psychotic state. Neither was expected to recover," said the sheriff grimly. Again, Maeve nodded. She was becoming anxious and recalled the guilt she felt after her last meeting with the sheriff when he blamed her for both men's tragic conditions. "Well, Maeve, I am delighted to report that the day after Samhain ended, both men miraculously began to improve! Deputy Henry's wounds have healed, and he is conscious and sitting up in bed. We expect him to return home in a few days!"

"Oh, my!" whispered Maeve. "And Deputy Don?" She was almost afraid of the answer.

"He has made an incredible recovery as well," said the sheriff, gleefully. "He's stable, off medication, and seems back to his normal self! He, too, will be returning home in about a week." The sheriff couldn't contain his joy.

Maeve began to cry tears of relief.

The sheriff said, "I wanted to come here in person and tell you myself. I'm sorry for the way I acted the last time I saw you."

"I understand, Sheriff Zen. You were right to be upset, and I was wrong to keep the information that I had from you. I'm sorry, too."

Maeve's father listened carefully to the conversation. He realized that there were things that had happened earlier that he was not privy to. "I'm truly happy to hear of your deputies' recovery, Sheriff. You are very fond of them. They're good men."

"Yes," agreed the sheriff, with a tear in the corner of his eye. "Well, I'll take my leave then. I just wanted Maeve to know the good news." The sheriff rose and left the Newell house.

James Newell looked at his daughter and said, "I guess there's a lot I've missed, Maeve. I've been so focused on my own needs."

At that point, Maeve sat down with her father on their threadbare couch, and she proceeded to fill him in on everything that had happened this past year. It was a long conversation, well overdue. Her father was amazed at his daughter's courage and determination in extreme circumstances. He was also very glad of Maeve's friendship with Sylvie, whom he considered a fine influence on Maeve. Additionally, he was impressed with what he learned about Nelda. There was so much to her that he hadn't been aware of, and he understood why his Alice was as close to her as she was.

"I guess I'm gonna' have to find some work to support us," said James. There's not much call for farmers or ranchers now. Wren Falls is beginning to expand, and new shops and buildings will become part of the scenery in the near future. I've always been handy. I built our home from scratch. I've got some skills, so maybe I'll start my own construction company—get a jump on any building that's gonna' happen around here." He rubbed his chin as he considered the idea.

"That's a great idea, Pa!" Maeve agreed. "By the way, I expect Grandpa's house will be coming down in two weeks. What's going to happen to that property?"

"Well, Maeve. I've been givin' that a lot of thought. The buyers of the property are a group of doctors. They want to see a medical center in the heart of Wren Falls. I think we need one that can serve the needs of our residents, more than we need more houses or stores. What if I take half the money I'll get for the property and donate it to a new Wren Falls medical center? The other half I can use to build us a brand-new home and save some for your future, whatever your plans. Does that seem fair, Maeve??"

"I think that's a terrific idea!" said Maeve. "That way, people like Deputy Henry and Deputy Don wouldn't have to go to the next town to get medical treatment. They could be taken care of right here in Wren Falls and having a new home for ourselves would be a dream come true!"

"Yeah," said Pa, I think it's time we got out of this place into a new home and started the next chapter of our lives together. As far as the medical center is concerned, we could have doctors who take care of every part of a person's body and surgeons, too. What do you think we should call the medical center, Maeve? Since I'm donatin' such a lot of money, they told me I could choose its name. How 'bout that??"

"Hmm. Let me think," pondered Maeve. After a few minutes, she yelled, "I've got it! We'll call it the Alice Newell Memorial Medical Arts Building! How do you like that, Pa?"

James Newell turned to his daughter's excited face and, in a voice breaking with emotion, said, "I like it, Maeve. I like it just fine."

Maeve looked at her father with renewed affection. "I didn't think we'd get to this point in our relationship, Dad, I've missed you."

James put his arms around his daughter and gave her a kiss on her forehead. "I've missed you, too, honey. This is a new beginning for the two of us."

Pooch barked at the two of them.

"I mean the three of us," added James, laughing at Pooch. "Just one big happy family at last."

Epilogue

What's Happening in Wren Falls Now?

Eight years later...

James Newell, construction foreman and owner of his company, Wren Falls Construction Co., completes the Alice Newell Memorial Medical Arts Building and is now working on several other projects in the area. His company is thriving, and the townspeople regard him with new respect. Several decrepit properties in the town have been razed and renovated by James. His reputation for doing outstanding work has spread throughout Wren Falls. He has not touched a drop of whiskey since the events of Halloween and is getting help for his alcohol addiction. James is now seven months sober and has completely dismantled his makeshift still.

However, he is not too busy to spend time with his daughter, Maeve. Their relationship is blossoming, and she is no longer invisible to him. In her limited spare time, Maeve accompanies her father to job sites, assists the crew, conveys directions from her dad, and helps out with small construction tasks.

Maeve finishes high school and becomes a paranormal investigator, traveling around the country to solve mysterious cases. Pooch accompanies her on her journeys, providing an early warning system when necessary, and an emotional support partner when required. Between jobs, James often travels with Maeve and enjoys seeing unfamiliar places in the country. He can be seen taking care of Pooch on these trips when Maeve is involved in her paranormal investigations. Maeve now has an impressive reputation for solving unnatural mysteries and enjoys the work thoroughly.

Maeve and Sylvie are still best friends and connect often by phone or through their dreams. Maeve's connection with Aunt Nelda remains close Her relationship with her father is the best it has been since before Alice's death.

Aunt Nelda is now an alternative medicine specialist in the new medical building, where she practices her unusual methods of healing. The people of Wren Falls love her and appreciate her skills. She is known for her success rate in curing Wren Falls' residents of whatever ails them.

Nelda is very friendly with an older gentleman who assists her in creating potions and medications. He is about her age, and the two appear very compatible. Neighbors wonder if the relationship will become permanent. Nelda still dabbles in Light Magic, but saves those occasions for the people closest to her. There are no complaints to date about her unusual activities.

Sylvie goes to art school and becomes a commercial artist for an organization that promotes the preservation of wildlife, particularly endangered species. She is very concerned with preserving the environment and its inhabitants. Sylvie is a Light Witch in training with Aunt Nelda and frequently consults with Maeve on her more challenging cases. Sylvie's father is now aware of her interest in magic and is accepting of it although his change of attitude is slow in coming.

Deputy Don is completely recovered and enjoying life with his wife and three children—two daughters and a son. He is retired from the force and is taking classes to become a physician's assistant, while his wife teaches at the local elementary school. For Don, this is another way to serve his community. Since his catastrophic health crisis, he is much more concerned with the health of his community. The family enjoys skiing in the winter on Hunter Mountain and tubing in the summer on rivers and lakes. The children are well-versed in first aid techniques.

Deputy Henry is also fully recovered. He, too, is retired from the police force and is happily married to a lovely young woman. He has two sons.

Henry is the owner of a successful auto body shop. He enjoys hunting for deer in the fall with the sheriff and dancing with his wife at local town get-togethers. He is careful not to go too deeply into the surrounding woods when deer-hunting.

Sheriff Zen is retired, too. He enjoys a quieter existence with his spouse, gardening and fishing. The sheriff takes ballroom dancing lessons with his wife and recently went on a second honeymoon with her to Niagara Falls. He is happy to put the past behind him.

Wren Falls experiences a facelift with all the new buildings and shops in the area. The town becomes a tourist destination again, owing to better weather conditions for skiing, ice skating, and fishing. The state wildlife commission stocks the local rivers and lakes with trout each year, since rain is now plentiful in the region. The reservoirs, lakes, and rivers are full, and no dry creek beds are visible in the area. Many year-round residents of other regions in the state relocate to Wren Falls as they flee more congested areas. The town is unrecognizable from its former appearance.

Residents of Wren Falls no longer find ravens in the town or its environs. Morrigan and her followers reside elsewhere. Perhaps in your town?

The Codex Demonicus remains hidden in a locked trunk in Nelda's basement. She is unwilling to open the trunk ever again. *The Encyclopedia of Celtic Lore* occupies prominent shelf space in her private library. Maeve and Sylvie have no plans to read the old Celtic stories in the near future. The two friends are pleased to know the book is in safe-keeping at Nelda's house. They are relieved to put the whole Wren Falls mystery behind them.

At least, for now...

CHECK OUT THESE OTHER GREAT ROWAN PROSE BOOKS:

Anne Wolf's writing career began with her first scribbling "A TOE" at the age of four on her mother's dining room wall. She was enthralled with her written work. Her mother, not so much. It was the beginning of Anne's foray into written and spoken language. This led her to study several languages, and teach integrated language arts and history (including ancient cultures and myths) to middle school-aged students. Throughout her career, she wrote several poems, essays, short stories, and picture books as models for her students. She received a mini-grant from the New York State English Council for her multicultural teaching unit. Anne still teaches creative writing classes in neighboring communities. She resides on Long Island with her family. THE TELLING is her debut YA Thriller novel.